Time Well Spent

by

the Grosmont Writers' Group

GWG

www.antonywootten.co.uk

GWG is an imprint of
Eskdale Publishing, UK

First published in Great Britain in 2013 by Eskdale
Publishing, North Yorkshire

A Catalogue record for this book is available from the British
Library.

ISBN: 978-0-9537123-6-6

Printed and bound in the UK by
York Publishing Services
www.yps-publishing.co.uk

Grosmont Writers' Group

I started the group less than a year ago, with the aim of getting together with like-minded writers who want to help each other hone their skills. I had not realised how exciting that process would be, and what great friends I would make. I love the fact that we represent such an eclectic mix of styles, interests and literary genres. Our meetings are about listening to each other read what we've written, and then telling each other what we think of it! Honest criticism can be tough to take, but a glass of home-made wine, or a pint of local ale and the friendly atmosphere of a member's house, or the Crossing Club in Grosmont where we have often met, help to make the process easier. It's very rare that we descend into full-blown fist fights anyway.

Each meeting, we are treated to historical novels, modern day thrillers, wildly obscure fantasies, real-life memoirs, and thought-provoking tales of every-day life. And each is a glimpse into another world, the world inside a writer's mind. These are always surprising and inspiring places. This book is a chance for us to share with you some of that wonderful variety. We believe that reading it certainly will be time well spent.

Antony Wootten

Contents

The Boss

Caroline Stewart

He glanced up at the clock. 'Oh Christ,' he cursed. The Boss would be back soon and he hadn't finished all of the work he'd been given to do that day. He'd be in big trouble. When The Boss gave you something to do you did it or you suffered the consequences which were often painful and never pleasant.

He took a breath and decided to go all-out to get everything done. Inside he knew it was an impossible task. There was simply too much to do and unfortunately for him The Boss was always punctual. He sighed as he recalled wasting two hours of the morning trying to solve some stupid problem with his PC. It needed doing but it wasn't on his list of jobs as dictated by The Boss. It would be no defence. He resigned himself to his inevitable fate.

He heard the key in the lock and his heart sank.

The Boss was back.

She walked in, her angry eyes blazing as she

surveyed the room.

'Hello Darling. Have you had a good day at work?' he asked meekly.

Without even looking at him she raised her left arm and struck him across the side of his head with the back of her hand. 'You haven't finished the ironing. One simple thing I ask you to do to help me and you can't even be bothered to do that.'

Then she smiled and said sweetly, 'What's for dinner?'

Crow Tree

Tamsyn Naylor

There was a rustle at the entrance, a rustle of smooth, black satin as the light dimmed in the place. What had been a strange, still silence became animated as the figures inside reacted to the arrival. The charcoal grey feathers on the floor rose and formed into pleading, insistent, gaping beaks. The bird had brought a large moth; the wings encased its beak and the soft hairs of its body glistened against the shaft of sun shining in through the hole.

The chicks pulled and climbed to reach the small morsel, but it was not enough to go round and as the bird left there was a slow disappointing sink back into resignation.

Some time later the place went dark again as the other parent bird entered, this time with a rodent hanging from its mouth. The tail hung limp and tempting. As the chicks again heaved there was an unsettling movement as a gaze was cast towards the helpless body. The eyes felt every being that was brought for consumption; after all, in many cases it had been the fate of their host. As the flesh of the pitiful corpse was greedily torn apart, the sadness showed in the eyes that surrounded the inside of the nest hole, eyes that had been brought there by the curious crows to line the inside of their lair, eyes that they had been drawn to from every dead animal the birds had found, while scanning the fields from above.

For many years now, every time the crows had landed to investigate a recently killed body, they had been attracted to the reflection in the dead face. They would hop round and look into the eye for some time and want it, want it for themselves to look at and admire. Pulling at the delicate socket area and snapping the sinew from the skull, the eye would be released for the bird to take, the inside of the nest hole being the perfect place to hide it from predators, but also to admire it. The wall of eyes was protection, watching over the young as they grew, looking out for them.

Some were from sheep, some from wild creatures: badgers, rabbits and stoats, squinting in the differing light; other birds: the owl, pigeons, moorhens, scanning the space, flitting from the opening to the floor; some from horses and deer, soulful and deep.

The eyes still saw everything, still felt emotion, were still aware, but they could not communicate, could not cry out, and could not stop what was happening.

The rodent was now gone, the commotion on the nest subsided and the eyes dropped again, some sleeping, some just reflecting.

The crows returned several more times that afternoon, each time satisfying the craving of the mouths. As the day wore on, the clouds outside of the hole gathered and darkened and a strong breeze whipped the branches across the entrance. The strength of the wind increased, rumbling the tree and causing the plastic caught in the fence outside to flap furiously like a huge, terrified flock of pigeons after a gun shot. The first few drops of rain fell as the storm approached, a crack of thunder hinting at what was to come. Minutes later the sky broke open with an almighty tear as the air shook, the tree creaked and groaned with the force and the sky danced with static. The chicks were highly agitated, pinning themselves to the floor and circling in panic. All of the eyes were alert and excited, dancing glances around in a frenzy.

In a split second the whole of the inside of the nest was alive with a searing light. The eyes all turned at once, mesmerised, to the hole. The tree splintered and broke open at the crown; a flame flushed through the branches, sending a shower of dancing sparks onto the loose nest material, which quickly caught alight. The birds panicked and scrambled over and over each other, reaching for the daylight.

The flames took hold, dancing wildly in slender

plumes, higher and higher. The eyes watched, flashing and fast, darting glances to each other as the flames reflected back from them. The whole place was intensely hot, wetness dripped onto the wall, creating a macabre scene.

One of the birds managed to get to the entrance and lingered momentarily before plunging out. The others could not scrabble high enough and quickly became lethargic, changing to still as the smoke overtook them, smoke that broke up the shafts of moonlight that now shone out from the un-obscured sky.

The sight was now calmed; wisps wound their way out of the ravaged trunk of the destroyed tree. Nothing remained of the nest site when the crows returned. They perched in a twisted branch, surveying the scene. On the ground beneath them, they could just make out a lifeless form.

A magpie, attracted by the commotion, had flown down with a bounced landing, next to the body. It hopped around and turned back again surveying the corpse with its head cocked. A moment later it bent forward, pecking at the side of the head. Only a few tugs and it was rewarded with its prize, before flying off to its roost.

Purple Shoes

Melanie Allanson

Alex danced self consciously, aware of his lack of skill in this area. He felt clumpy and uncoordinated. Across the floor he saw several girls, but one in particular caught his eye. Five foot eight, at a guess, dark-haired and natural-looking with a cheeky, raucous laugh when she was talking to the gaggle of girls around her. She stood out amongst them, especially as she was a head above them all in high, dark purple stilettos. She had her arms raised above her head, eyes closed, and was swaying her sexy hips to the music. He had been to Siren's nightclub on very few occasions, not being a fan of one night stands and having already shed one wife he had met here. Now, divorced, he felt lonely and, looking over at this lovely creature, he felt the hope that there might be someone who could make him happy. His usual evenings were spent watching crime dramas with a bottle of Budweiser in hand. Not that he really minded his own company, better than being with the wrong woman, and he quite liked to please himself.

She was coming over; his hands felt clammy. He had to get this right. 'Er ... Hello ...' he stammered.

She smiled at him and he realised what a fool he was as she was clearly headed in the direction of the tall, good-looking guy behind him. They cut a handsome couple, a good match. Alex caught a whiff of her perfume as she moved past him and he could not help but stare at her.

He took her all in now that she was facing the other way. She was wearing sparkly tights which displayed shapely legs and a tiny denim mini skirt with a vest top. She had lovely, soft-looking skin and a way of acting as if the person she was talking to was the only person that mattered. He wished she would give him her attention just for a moment. She swished her hair around as she talked animatedly, clearly having a heated discussion. He was trying to work out whether this was her boyfriend or not. Not that it really mattered, she was well out of his league.

Just then, Jim, his work-partner, sauntered up to him and, catching him eyeing the girl, dug him playfully in the ribs.

'Hey mate, I think she's already taken!' They watched as the girl wound her arms around the lad's neck and turned away as they saw that she clearly only had eyes for him. Jim was fun and they had a laugh talking about work and his latest domestic dramas with wife-to-be, Jane. However, Alex was only listening with one ear, still trying to tune into the couple's conversation. He only caught snippets through the maelstrom of music and voices around him, but he got the gist: the plan was they were going to get hold of some drugs, then go back to hers. No need to guess where that little scenario would end. Anyway, not any of his business, he was off-duty and they were old enough to take care of themselves. Shame though, because she was lovely.

The rest of the evening was spent chatting to some older ladies and having a bit of banter with them. He had fun and had almost forgotten the girl until he saw her leaving, arm in arm with the guy, clearly both very drunk.

*

It was the following morning when Alex and Jim got a call to attend a road traffic accident. They were the nearest to the junction and sped off towards the queue of traffic building in front of them. They took to the hard shoulder, sirens blaring, at eighty miles per hour. They soon reached the carnage, and the young policemen saw, all over the carriage way, the debris from an upturned car and a shattered motorbike. It was a bad one. The two men quickly joined the first-responder who was crouching beside the apparently lifeless body of the motorcyclist.

Looking up, the first responder began to direct them towards the wreckage of the car, telling them about what he'd found. He used words like 'fatality' and 'deceased', but Alex's attention was drawn by the sight of something lying in the road amongst the debris. In the distance, he could hear the ambulances' sirens wailing. Head reeling, he bent to pick up the object: a single, purple stiletto.

Everything and Nothing

Paula Harrison

It was a beautiful morning for a ride. I saddled up my dependable, reliable, faithful old pony and set off across the moor. We were a good team, having enjoyed time together over many years. We knew each other's moods and idiosyncrasies. I needed that pony. He was my escape from the twenty-first century into another world. The sun was warm on my shoulders and a gentle breeze blew. The lambs were growing up and the heather was beginning to bloom. I liked the grass tracks of the moor. We increased our pace. As I glanced down, it seemed the ground was rushing by at ninety miles an hour. We steadied our pace over the rough ground and as we reached a gate we stood for a moment. There were no twenty-first century sounds. We listened to the silence broken only by the high-pitched sound of golden plovers and lapwings circling above their nests. We continued down the valley and across the river. I loved my days off from work. I loved my riding. I always did a lot of thinking while on my pony, thinking of nothing in particular.

Across the river - no problem for my old pony - we carried on up a steep slope through the woods, emerging onto the public bridleway that covered the final four hundred yards to the farm. I dawdled for a moment at the gate, looking back at where we had just ridden. I had completed this ride many times over the past thirty years and it was my favourite: no roads, just open moorland and fantastic views.

I was jerked back to reality by a loud, aggressive, threatening voice shouting, 'What the hell are you doing on my land? Get the hell out of here.'

Vibs, my pony, looked, his ears twitching like radar.

'Professionalism,' I thought, even though it was my day off work. I replied, 'Who are you and what gives you the right to speak to me like that? I'm not some peasant; the feudal system died years ago. I made sure that I was through the gate and I am on a public bridleway: that's what the blue arrows mean. Surely you must be aware of the many rights of way that cross your land.'

I thought he was going to burst. I got the impression that people in the past had not stood up to him. He reminded me of an overweight bull, stamping, angry, the veins standing out on his neck and his eyes bulging.

'Get off my land and don't come back,' he

shouted.

'Oh! I'll be back - it's a regular ride,' I replied.

'I'll put fencing up. I'll see you off,' was his final threat.

'Oh! fine,' I thought as I went back to the farm.

Going through the farm gates, Bill was there.

'I heard shouting,' he said. 'I meant to warn you about him before you left but you'd gone before I had chance. He told me not to shift the sheep along the access road.'

'Who is he anyway, speaking to us peasants like that?' I asked.

Bill laughed. 'I think you might have summat there. He's taken over the tenancy two days ago and already got a reputation.'

'Not on our wavelength, Bill. He's a lot of learning to do,' I said.

I brushed Vibs, picked out his hooves, put on the hoof oil and led him to his field. I watched him from the gate peacefully grazing.

*

Two days later at work, where the banter in the A & E changing rooms was always good, I pinned on my name badge and put my food in the fridge. We had a few moments before the shift began so I told the staff on shift about the incident on the bridle-path and being spoken to as if I were a peasant. They all laughed. We took over from the night staff. Chris, the boss, asked, 'Right, Peasant, can you go and check Resus?'

I'd checked Bay One and Chris came back in.

'I've just taken an ambulance call. Chap with chest pain, can I leave it with you, Peasant?' she asked.

'How long, Chris?'

'Twenty minutes,' she replied.

I liked a few moments to arrange the monitors, open the drugs cupboard and run intravenous fluids through necessary apparatus. The student nurse came through and asked if she could stay. I explained what I was doing.

She said, 'We're all having a good laugh out there about you being a peasant.'

'Good,' I said. 'I like laughter.'

I heard the ambulance reversing.

'Come on, Tez, let's get these doors open,' I commanded.

The crew appeared with an overweight, grey, clammy patient struggling to breathe.

'Tez, can you let the doctor and anaesthetist know that the patient is here?' I asked.

We transferred him to the trolley, attached the monitors and got him comfortable. We administered pain relief. I took a handover from the crew. They gave me the history.

'That arrogant devil wants private care. We explained that private hospitals don't have A & E Departments so he is stuck here with you lot,' commented the paramedic.

'Peasants,' I heard whispered in the background. I suppressed a smile. The story had obviously travelled. Dr Khan and I shot each other a glance knowing that neither of us liked the look of the heart trace on the monitor.

'Hey, Peasant, sort the drugs can you?' requested the doctor.

I saw Tez and the other doctors smirking. I attached the syringe driver and looked at the patient again.

'I don't believe this,' I thought. My own heart missed a beat. He was starting to settle now and I had a few moments to update my writing. I looked at the ambulance form. Yes, the address and details matched up.

Chris came in. 'Are you lot OK?' she asked.

I explained quickly about the situation in which I found myself. Luckily he didn't recognise me. 'Oh Chris, where it says 'patient condition' can I write 'arrogant devil'?'

Tez smiled, probably wondering what kind of emergency department she'd come to.

'Get on, Peasant,' Chris grinned and left.

Once we got him stabilised and comfortable, he managed to say, 'Who are you people?' I explained what had happened to him, the monitors, his treatment and the plan when he left Resus. I asked if there was anything that he needed and if he'd like to see his wife. Once in, her first words were, 'We usually have private care.' She looked around Resus. 'You staff seem to know what you're doing.' She sat by her husband. Not very much was said. We asked if she needed anything. She seemed lost in a world of her own. After a few moments she said that they had just moved and that she thought it may have been a mistake. I daren't let on what I knew. 'This is the last straw. We don't know anybody,' she volunteered.

'Give yourself time.'

The phone rang. 'A bed is ready on Coronary Care.' I explained that we'd be transferring her husband to Coronary Care and that she could go with him.

*

The weeks passed by until there was a hint of autumn in the air. The village shows had all finished and the heather was past its best. I saddled up Vibs. Bill shouted, 'Where are you going today, Peasant?'

'I think I'll do my favourite ride over the moor,' I laughed back at him.

I did my favourite ride over the moor, stopping occasionally to listen to the silence. I knew what was important in life. Up here there was nothing and yet there was everything - big skies, open space, birds and silence from the outside world. I came through the wood to the last field feeling like I was riding through ancient history. There were the old trods used by the medieval monks and traders and I briefly thought about those who had walked here before me.

I arrived at the last gate and saw a bent, frail-looking old man.

'Good morning,' I said. He looked at me through sunken eyes, leaning on a stick and very breathless. He just stared. I looked again and as I spoke his wife appeared. I recognised her immediately. Rather haughtily she said, 'You ride over here regularly, don't you? It's our property now.'

I thought, 'Here we go again ...' I reminded her that the blue arrows signified a public bridle-path and that I would continue to use it on a daily basis. I tried to make light of the situation, explaining that I had lived in these parts all of my life and if, in years to come, there was a ghost riding on a black and white pony, it would be me. I immediately felt a silent, unfriendly hostility.

'How is your husband now?' I ventured to ask.

'What do you know about it?' she snapped.

'I know because I am the nurse on the team who looked after your husband in the resuscitation area,' I answered. Her face fell, there was a stunned silence. 'There is a way of living here you know. The natives are friendly. You don't have to be so hostile and bitter. You took on the tenancy. It's a small community, and for it to work well there has to be give and take,' I explained to her.

'Reg,' she called sharply to him. I felt strangely sorry for him, a shadow now of an old man. I took Vibs over to him.

'Do you like horses?' I asked.

'Yes,' he answered feebly.

'Reg, this lass looked after you in hospital,' his wife told him, and his face fell.

'You were a good lot. I was well cared for. Do you enjoy living here?' he queried.

'It's like living in heaven.' As I left I felt they were staring at me going over the field.

'Hey. Peasant, I see you're back,' shouted Bill.

'Yes,' I said thoughtfully. 'I've just seen that arrogant devil and his wife again.'

'So?' said Bill.

'I felt a bit sorry for them.'

'Oh, come off it you soft sod. The way he spoke to you, me and everyone else,' Bill said, rather unsympathetically.

I looked at Bill and said, 'Well, they may have all the money in the world but he has been ill. They are just an isolated, lonely pair.'

'Come on, Peasant, get that pony sorted, then give us a hand with these sheep,' said a smiling Bill.

On my way back home, my thoughts wondered back to the old man and his wife. I had to pass the house again and saw that they were alone in the garden. I called to them. They beckoned me over and I asked if they would like me to bring the pony to see them again. They said that they would and they invited me to join them for a drink. I remarked that their garden was a peaceful haven and a pleasure in which to sit. They said that they were settling into their new home and enjoying what was on offer. On leaving, I said that I think we have both found new friends.

The Cad

Josephine Esterling

Margarita sipped her cocktail, its bitter-sweet taste lingering in her mouth. She looked across the small balcony table at the woman in pink and admired her daring. Her dress was cut low at the back and sides, revealing, in Margarita's mind, a little too much flesh even for the nineteen-twenties. Earlier she had caught a glimpse of the younger woman's thigh as the generous folds of the paler pink skirt had revealed a slit up the side of the fabric while Johanna had been dancing with James.

Margarita felt a tinge of jealousy. James had barely spoken to her all evening. Oh yes he had played the part of the charming suitor when she arrived, and he'd had her accompany him while he greeted each of his guests. But, as soon as the party was in full swing he had off-loaded her, conveniently she thought, on to one of his associates. Margarita sighed, the peck on the cheek and whispered promises had made her think perhaps he would return for her later in the evening. But, as soon as Johanna had arrived in a flurry of pink silk and white ermine fur, she knew she would be second best. And that was before James' announcement, which changed everything.

She knew now that she should have told him about the baby sooner. She touched her stomach. She was glad of the matching green chiffon crepe shawl that she had fashionably wound around the top half of her black and green evening dress, with the ends hanging down over her stomach, although she was hardly showing yet, she thought. A six month 'holiday' in Hastings would help her avoid the scandal, but was she getting a little old, she wondered. The face in the mirror as she had applied her make-up before leaving her London flat had shown no tale of her coming birthday. Although thirty was no great age, the prospect of losing her youthful looks without a husband in tow, worried her. Besides, she thought, her money was dwindling.

'James is such a handsome chap,' Margarita said casually to Johanna.

'Yes, awfully,' the woman replied, 'and rich.'

'Yes, and he was single until now,' Margarita said. The two women looked at each other in the moonlight. 'Who is she anyway?' Johanna asked and noisily sipped her champagne.

'I have absolutely no idea,' Margarita replied.

'Arriving like that - I've never seen her in James' crowd before.'

'No, James and I ...' Margarita trailed off now unsure of what her position with James had actually been.

'I came along. Sorry,' Johanna said and finished her drink in one swift motion.

'Yes,' Margarita said, giving Johanna a cold stare, although she felt that she did not quite mean it. 'Now here we are,' she added.

'Yes,' said Johanna. 'Announcing his engagement like that, right out of the blue, the cad.'

'Yes, the cad.' Both women laughed.

'He would never have made a good father anyway,' Johanna sighed and smoothed down her dress, her hand lingering on her stomach.

'She is welcome to the cad,' they both agreed.

You Reap

What You Sow

Tamsyn Naylor

I miss my life ... I miss looking out of the window, sitting by the fire, pottering about, humming to myself as I went about my ordinary life. But that is far from ordinary now ...

It all started quite subtly, just a feeling something was different, not quite right. I would look out of the window as I dressed and glimpse, in the forming dewy mist creeping along the field, a slight movement, a shape merging into a shadow. The light was dim and shifting. Could it be a deer? It didn't move nimbly or gracefully, didn't really appear to be there at all.

A few days later, as I climbed the track behind my house, the sun beat down onto my shoulders, the ground smelt warm from the late summer rays penetrating through the trees. As I walked on, following the path of a hoverfly flitting between dandelion flowers, I heard a rustle, deep in the hedge. I knew there was something there, the faint cloud of its breath lit up against the damp vegetation. But I was alone ...

This uncertain feeling continued in my mind on several occasions after that.

The year was turning; the mornings were more crisp and clear. I was pulling seed heads out in the garden one day, when the pig lumbered into view. It was snuffling through the fallen leaves, looking for worms. That's strange, I thought, my neighbour would normally have told me if she was getting more livestock. It was not alone, there were four or five, all different sizes but all intent on their grubbing. Two more appeared in the following week, gentle creatures. I didn't see my neighbour, didn't get the chance to ask her about the additions.

I spent a precious hour in the garden – tidying up before winter. As I pushed the barrow of deads through the gate to the compost corner, I was startled to see the rough, turned over, exposed ground. Holes had appeared. In my pause I did not hear them coming. I jolted as the gate smashed against the back of my legs, powered by the combined force of several large pigs gambolling into the field. I fell onto the bare sticky earth, cracking my skull on the corner of my barrow as I went, and lay motionless and limp. I sank into a dark sleep.

The pigs carried on scurrying and romping, pulling at my clothes. As they scuffed under my arms and sides, the soil started to slip and move, swallowing me into the damp, leafy loam.

*

Winter came and the last of the leaves fluttered from the trees. I consciously felt the first frost and knew that after all this time I needed to fill my belly with something. Moving over to the hedge, I slumped down onto the ground with tiredness and waited, waited for a morsel to pass me and quench my hunger. After quite some time had passed and a watery sun had sunk below the level of the hill, a creature approached. As it passed the hedge, a hair's breadth away from me, I clearly saw it carried something in its mouth. I couldn't make it out – was it meat, a limp lifeless body? No, it was stiff and pearlescent, a furless morsel.

As the dog stopped, it carefully dropped its prey and began to dig. I recognised the dog as my own, my faithful happy friend who loved me beyond all else. The many times, whilst out shopping, I recollected her smiling loyal eyes and was reminded to bring her home her favourite: a pig's ear. But when, I thought, had I ever seen her eat them? Take them, yes, and relish them, laying in the hall with the treat placed between her paws, coveting them.

As I watched, the horror of the realisation dawned on me. They were my treats; they were my pigs, planted by my own dog. My breath was panicky, I could not shout. I fell onto the damp earth and watched in horror as my dog covered over the ear, planting the seed of my destiny, and trotted back up the field and into the comfort of my old home.

Sanctuary

Ray Stewart

She looked around at her family. She had to get away as she imagined their eyes prying into her soul. She had a secret, a secret that she could share with no-one. 'I'm going for a walk,' she said. 'I won't be too long.'

She opened the door and stepped out into a fine August afternoon. The village was about a mile away from the cottage but she turned away and headed in the direction of open country.

Her head reeled. How many weeks had it had been? She looked at the cloudless sky and listened to the birds singing their cheerful songs. She thought back to *that* night and then shut it out again, the guilt tearing at her heart. She walked along, the hot sun burning her back. She wished that she'd brought a hat along. She would suffer before this afternoon was over.

She noticed a lane to the left of the main road and turned down it, descending a steep twisting path. As she reached the bottom of the incline, her isolation was broken by a BT van tucked in close to the dry stone wall. At the top of a telegraph pole was a man with tools belted around his waist as he worked on one of the lines. She craved isolation but he spoke to her.

'Afternoon. What a lovely day, for a change.'

'Afternoon,' she replied. 'Yes, summer is here at last.' She kept it short and perhaps not so sweet. She wanted no conversation, no words... that was how it had all started. Silence, apart from the singing of the birds and the rustling of the trees... and isolation. Yes, that was what she wanted.

She tried to blank her thoughts from her mind, but they would not let go of her. She looked at the sheep in the fields unbothered by her passing and she envied them. Reaching the bottom of the incline she looked upwards to see an even steeper gradient to tackle. She set off at a brisk pace which lessened as the back of her shirt darkened with perspiration.

How had it happened? She had known him for about four years. They were good friends. They enjoyed each other's company. She winced when she remembered how angry she had been when he turned up late for a meeting at work, and how he had tried to win her around by buying her a strawberry tart at lunchtime. It had worked. They sat at the foot of the market cross, and ate and talked as they normally did, her anger gone.

She reached another junction, turned right and headed towards a roadside pub. The afternoon was passing and her recent exertions in climbing the bank had created a thirst in her. She walked along, the slight breeze slowly drying her damp shirt. The odd car passed her but the occupants were as engrossed in their own little worlds as she was in trying to escape from hers. She wished there was someone she could talk to but there was no-one that she could rely upon to understand her situation. She recalled *that* night when they had both been away on conference duties. They had stayed at a small place out of town, an isolated inn at the end of a country lane. They had sat with colleagues talking about the day's business long into the night. He had been there. She was watching the clock, silently longing for everyone to go to bed so that they could have a few minutes on their own. Eventually, after midnight, they were left alone with a tired, 'See you two in the morning.' They were comfortable with each other and enjoying each other's company. This was definitely the best part of the evening.

A car honked at her as she approached the pub, awakening her from her memories. The pub was welcoming. She ordered a drink, sitting outside, savouring the coldness of the glass. An old couple said a polite, 'Hello,' as she sat near them and she smiled back, not wanting to engage in conversation.

She drifted back to that night and remembered with a mixture of pleasure and guilt, how happy she was to be alone with this man. There was no danger or hidden agenda with him. He was married and so was she. Nothing was going to happen between them. He had said, 'It's nearly one. I suppose we should turn in.'

'Yes. I suppose we had better be at least half awake for tomorrow's business.'

'I think I'll take a little stroll down the lane before bed,' he had said. 'It might make it easier for me to settle down to sleep.'

She couldn't stop the words from coming out of her mouth. 'I'll come with you if you like.'

They opened the door and, stepping out into the darkness, started to stroll along the lane. It was a moonless, starless night and she slipped her right arm around his waist. He responded by putting his left arm gently around her shoulder and pulling her closer to him. They had only walked for what seemed to be a few yards when she became conscious of him lightly kissing her head and teasing her hair with his mouth. They stopped.

He lifted her face up to meet his and they began to kiss passionately. He pulled her closer to him and, noticing his arousal, she stopped him, saying, 'I'm a married woman. I know what that is.'

They walked back to the inn but did not say 'goodnight'. The downstairs of the inn was deserted by this time and he led her gently into a side room.

'Excuse me,' said a stranger, interrupting her reverie. 'Which way is it to Middleton?'

'Oh! Go on about another three miles and look

for a right turn signposted 'Cotherstone'. It's about two miles past Cotherstone,' she replied.

Stirred from her reflections, she looked at her glass and, leaving it, set off to return to the cottage. The sun was sinking in the sky and she realised that it would be dark when she returned. With an intensity in her pace she set off. Another mile, another right turn and then just follow the road to the cottage. How long had she been walking? How would she explain the long absence? A rough estimation told her that she must have walked about twelve miles since she had left, supposedly to clear her head.

She tried to shut the thoughts of that evening out of her consciousness but as she was walking along they returned to taunt her. Much to her annoyance she found herself enjoying the memories of that evening.

Entering the side room, he had sat down and pulled her upon his knee. The kissing started again and she stroked his face as his hand unbuttoned her top. She should have resisted but she let his hand explore her body. He pulled her shirt open and began kissing her breasts. His hand wandered lower and that was when responsibility kicked in and she stopped him. They looked into each other's eyes. 'Do you think you could ever love me?' she asked.

'Very easily,' he had replied with a smile in his eyes. 'Do you think *you* could ever love *me*?' he retaliated.

Again she couldn't stop the words tumbling from her mouth. 'I've loved you for the past four years,' she said, kissing him again.

The cottage hove into view, lights burning from the windows. What was she going to say? They knew that she had something on her mind and that she needed some space. Perhaps that would do. She entered the warm room, a chill now settling in for the night. She looked at Kieron and her children.

'Hello,' he said, 'we were getting worried about you. Are you feeling any better?'

'Sorry. I totally lost track of time. Yes, the fresh air has helped to clear my head,' she replied looking at the children and not at Kieron. 'I'm tired. I think I'll go straight up to bed,' she said.

'I'll bring you a cup of tea up,' he offered.

'Thanks,' she smiled, 'but I think I'll just go straight to sleep.'

She was aware of his presence as he entered the room but feigned sleep. He slipped into the bed silently behind her, kissing her shoulder gently before turning away. She silently cried when she remembered her unsaid wish that he would not return from work. That would have been so simple. Decision-making taken from her. She loved her husband, but she wanted someone else now, emotionally and physically.

She thought, or *tried* to think logically about the situation. She wondered if it was the excitement of being with someone new compared to the banality of her everyday life with Kieron that had made him seem so attractive to her, or was there really something deeper?

She could not bear to lose the love of this other man. But she could not bear to see her family torn apart either. So she would be forced to live a double life, one as the doting wife and mother, the other a secret life. With this resolution in her mind she closed her eyes and retreated to the sanctuary of sleep.

Me and Robbie

Antony Wootten

I love my Robbie. He's so brave. I'll tell you about the brave thing he did and what happened next, and what happened after that too.

We was walking past Kentucky Fried Chicken when we saw that boy who lives above us. He was a nasty piece of work, you could tell. He'd only lived there a few days. He always got his hood up, and always looked like he'd been in a fight, and he got things tattooed on his knuckles. Words. I didn't know what they said, I never got close enough to read them. I'm not very good at reading anyway. I'm better than my Robbie though. But that's ok because he's the brave one.

The boy, the one with the hood and the tattoos, he never liked us. He always looked at us as if we smell bad. We don't; we always wash and shower just like we were taught. Just because we got learning difficulties doesn't mean we don't know how to keep clean. That boy, he looked at us as if we're horrible, Robbie and me. He's not the only one, lots of people did that. They always do. My mum tells me to ignore people like that. They may be able to read better than me and Robbie, but we're better than those people. That's what Liz Jones says too. But it makes me cross when those people are nasty to us because my Robbie's so kind. No-one should think he's a horrible person. I can be annoying, I know that, because I'm always giggling for no reason, and I sulk a lot too, and have tantrums. Robbie's just quiet and kind, and that's why I love him.

Anyway, there's another way you could tell that boy with the hood was nasty. He was horrible to his dog. It was a cute brown one that looked strong and gentle, but my mum and Liz Jones said it was one of those dangerous dogs. I don't think it was dangerous though. It always looked scared. It flinched when the boy shouted at it. And it got scars. I think the boy hurted it. That made me and Robbie hate that boy because we both love dogs, especially Robbie does.

When we went past the Kentucky we saw that boy and his dog. He was with his friends. They all looked as nasty as he was. They always laughed when they saw us coming. That makes me really cross. It's not Robbie's fault he walks funny. But that day, Robbie and me saw that boy drop half a Kentucky Fried Chicken on the pavement outside for his dog to eat. He didn't care about that dog. He should have given it dog food, not Kentucky Fried Chicken. And he said, 'Eat it,' like that, angry and mean. And the dog did, but it looked like it didn't want to, as if it knowed it shouldn't. And my

Robbie said, 'You shouldn't give that to a dog,' but Robbie's got a quiet voice, and he always looks at the floor and people can't always tell what he's saying. The boy said, 'What?' like that, cross. And his friends started to laugh and say things about us. I can't remember what but not nice things. 'Chicken bones are bad for dogs,' Robbie said. I was proud of Robbie then because it was like he wasn't scared of the boy even though he looked so rough and nasty and all his friends were there. The boy said, 'You'd know, Brain of Britain,' and his friend said, 'Can't you give *her* chicken then?' pointing to me. I knowed what he meant. He meant I was a dog, which is rude. And another boy said, 'Can't you give your girlfriend your bone?' and they all laughed at that a lot.

Me and Robbie kept on walking. I was holding Robbie's arm which made me feel safe. Robbie was looking at the pavement and saying things even I couldn't tell what they were. When we'd gone quite far, Robbie said, 'I hate them.' I knew what he meant. He hated them for being horrible to the dog. He said, 'I'm going to buy that dog off him.' I was excited. I love dogs and always wanted one. I started laughing and pulling on his arm but he just kept walking and saying things I couldn't hear properly. The cash machine was miles away and Robbie got out some money and then we went all the way back again to the Kentucky. But the boys were all gone. I sulked because I wanted us to have that dog.

When we were back home I kept thinking about that dog. I wanted to rescue it. That night we heard a horrible row coming from upstairs. That's where the boy lived. There was a lady there too. They always rowed. It was horrible to hear it. I thinked he hit her sometimes. Quite a lot actually. We could always hear them shouting at each other and screaming at each other, and the dog would bark at them. But sometimes you'd hear the poor dog yelp as if someone had hurt it. I said, 'That nasty boy, he's hitting his wife, and the dog gets stuck in to help her, and then he kicks it or something.' Me and my Robbie just cuddled. We didn't know what to do. They'd only lived there a week or two, but they were spoiling our happy home.

We loved our home, our little flat. We'd maked it all pretty by painting the walls and putting up pictures. People used to think we couldn't do it but we did, and I'm glad they used to think that because it maked it seem so exciting and nice when we did do it. We could say, 'There. We done it. Told you we could.' And we were really happy there. And my mum helped us, and that lady, Liz Jones, always came round to make sure we were doing okay. She was nice. But that boy living upstairs spoilt everything a bit. Me and Robbie felt sad listening to the poor dog getting hurt.

It was really bad that night. You could hear things breaking and the dog was barking like mad. Me and Robbie knowed the boy was going to hurt it if it didn't stop barking. Robbie said, 'We should do something.' He was right, we both knowed it but we couldn't think what to do. I said Mum had always said to ring her if we didn't know what to do about something, and Robbie said, 'She's out.'

'How do you know that?' I said.

'She told us that,' Robbie said. 'She told us on the 14th of March.' Robbie always remembers things like that, he does. Then he started telling me exactly what we were doing on the 14th of March, and I listened because the 14th of March was a nice day when we met my mum and Liz Jones in the park and had a nice walk and Liz Jones said it was the warmest day of the year so far. But the shouting and barking from upstairs made us remember the poor dog and the lady too. 'I'm going to phone my mum,' I said, and Robbie said, 'I just told you, she's out.'

'Oh yes,' I said. Then I decided to call Liz Jones instead. I rang her number, but I was embarrassed so I threw the phone to Robbie and I started to giggle for no reason. It wasn't funny, I was scared, so I don't know why I giggled. But Robbie isn't very good talking on the phone and he mumbled some things slowly. Even I couldn't really tell what he was saying. I was cross with him, and I taked the phone off him. I said, 'Liz Jones, it's Eleanor and Robbie. We're scared and we don't know what to do. The man upstairs is hurting his wife and his dog and we want to make it stop. Listen,' I said and I holded the phone up so she could hear the row. 'Can you come and make them stop?' Liz Jones didn't say anything, and I waited but she still didn't say anything, and then there was a beep. It was an answering machine. 'Why didn't you tell me it was an answering machine?' I said and Robbie said he did, but he didn't.

'Stay here,' Robbie told me.

'Where are you going?' I said. I was scared and I felt sick. I wanted to be near my Robbie.

'I'm going to look,' he said.

'To look where?' I said, but Robbie was already putting his shoes on. I tied up the laces for him and then I did mine. I had to tell him to wait, and he would have gone out of the door by himself if I hadn't grabbed his coat with my teeth while I tied up my laces. Then I went with him, holding his arm. I love Robbie's arms, they are not very long but they are thick and strong and I like to wrap both my arms around one of his when we walk along. It was hard that day though because Robbie was walking faster than normal, and he was swinging from side to side a lot. We went round the back of the flats and straight up to the next floor.

We were at the back of the block. All the flats had their own balcony that side. Robbie was brave. He didn't even think about the dangers, he just started climbing along the balconies. From one to the next. I called, 'Robbie, wait!' and I followed him. It was scary, really scary, because there was a gap between each balcony, and you could see right down to the ground. Robbie told me to go back but I wouldn't. I was scared back there on my own. I wanted to be with Robbie so I climbed along. I'm not very good at climbing so Robbie helped me, even though he wanted me to go back. He knowed I wouldn't go back though. Every time I climbed over, Robbie had to hold me and pull me by my trousers, and we both fell down. Every time! I giggled, but Robbie didn't. I was scared someone would see us but they didn't. It's funny the things some people keep on their balconies. One of them had two old washing machines and some rusty bikes. One of them had a rabbit hutch full of beer bottles.

When we got to the boy's balcony we could already hear the shouting and the dog barking. There was an ash tray on the balcony and a bowl of water for the dog. Robbie knocked it over when I fell on him. It maked a loud noise. We were scared. We looked in through the window. We could see into their flat. The boy was sitting on the sofa and the lady was shouting at him. We could hear the dog but couldn't see it. The boy had his head down and looked sad. He shouted some things without even looking at her. Then he got up and tried to get past the lady but she wouldn't let him go past. He turned around waving his hands. Then the lady pushed him really hard. He didn't fall over, but she started hitting him, really hard. She had gone mad. The boy didn't fight back, he just crouched down and curled up. Then the dog came towards him. It had been behind the sofa. It looked really scared but it was barking at the lady. She screamed at it and it went behind the sofa again, but it didn't stay there. The boy was trying to get up but the lady kicked him in the face. Then she broke a bowl on his back and he fell to the floor. The dog came out again to help the boy and the lady kicked it. It yowled and barked and she hit it with her hand.

That's when I realised my Robbie was opening the door. He went inside! I saw him in the kitchen, and I watched him going as quickly as he could into the lounge. The lady stopped hitting the boy and looked at my Robbie. Robbie went to help the boy get up. He ignored the lady shouting at him and telling him to get out. The dog came towards him. It was limping.

Then, the woman hit herself in the face. The boy tried to stop her, but she kept doing it. And then the police arrived. Robbie let them in. The lady's face was bleeding, and the police grabbed hold of the boy. The dog was barking and Robbie was trying to explain and no-one knowed what was going on. I was hiding on the balcony and didn't know what to do. I waited and waited. I was too scared to look. I crouched down and cried.

It was ages and ages before I looked in again. I'd been asleep a bit, and all the shouting had stopped. It was quiet. I didn't know what to do. Robbie had gone. They all had. I was too scared to climb back over the balconies and too scared to go through the house. I just didn't know what to do. And then I remembered I had my phone in my pocket. I rang my mum and she came and got me by going to the flat next door and helping me climb over the balcony.

I was so happy when I saw Robbie. The police had arrested him! He shouldn't have been in the boy's flat. But the police didn't understand what he was saying to them. So me and Mum went to the police station to explain. After that, they let Robbie and the boy go. I don't know where the dog had gone. The boy didn't say anything to us, he just went off in a car with his friends.

I don't think the boy went back to live at his flat after that. The lady did, I saw her. But I didn't see the boy or the dog after that. Not for ages. Not for a really long time. Then one day there was a knock at the door. Robbie opened it. Robbie always answered the door. I was always scared but Robbie wasn't. So Robbie opened the door and I held his arm.

It was the boy. He had his hood up, and he stamped out his cigarette on the pavement. He said, 'Alright?' We didn't know what to say. It was embarrassing a bit. The boy's dog was sitting next to him. The boy said, 'I never thanked you. You know, for helping me out.' Robbie nodded and looked at the floor. 'For helping us both out, me and my dog.' I knowed it would be polite to ask the boy in, but I was too shy. I tugged on Robbie's arm and tried to get him to do that but he didn't. 'Sorry about my mates, you know, the things they say to you sometimes. I've told them not to anymore. I told them you're alright.' Robbie nodded and I giggled. And I tugged on Robbie's arm and whispered to him to let the boy in. 'Anyway, I got you something to say thanks. It's from both of us, me and 'im.' The boy nodded towards the dog and the dog barked once. Then the boy picked up a box I hadn't seen. He gived it to Robbie. 'It's a puppy. My mate's dog had puppies and I thought you might like one. This dirty old bugger's the father!' His dog barked again. It was like the dog knew what the boy meant. Robbie said, 'Thanks,' and he gave me the box. I couldn't see because I was crying and I didn't know what to do. I just stood there. 'Have a look,' said the boy.

Robbie peered into the box. 'It's a puppy,' he said.

'I know that,' said the boy. 'D'you wan' 'im? He's for you. A present.'

'Yes please,' said Robbie. Then the boy came in and helped me put the box on the floor. The puppy was tiny and sleepy.

'I checked with your mum first,' the boy said. 'She says it's okay, she'll help you look after it.'

'And Liz Jones,' I said, because Liz Jones would help us too.

The boy gave us two small cans of dog food. 'So you don't have to give him Kentucky Fried Chicken,' he said, which was funny because that's what *we'd* told *him*.

The Mind Boggler

Tamsyn Naylor

The windows were smoky. I held my hand against the light to peer in through the glass. In the gloom there was an array of untidiness, cases and boxes stacked around in a disorderly way, the glint of brass from a well-rubbed handle around a heavy mahogany counter. I could see a figure, waistcoated with a small chain hanging from a pocket. A bell tinkled as I lifted the catch and pushed open the heavy door, the words 'Francis Fickleworth's' etched into the opaque glass. A familiar honey smell greeted me as I entered.

'Hello there, not seen you for a while,' he said as I approached the counter across the worn parquet floor.

'Yes, I haven't been in for some time now,' I laughed, thinking back to the times I had regularly called in during my teenage years.

'What can we do for you?'

There was a lady standing with her back towards me, tall and thin, her hair combed close to her head. She was surveying the small handwritten labels on the boxes stacked along the wall. Each box held a roll of parchment, tied with a ribbon inside, the writing on which could only be read by someone in need of its contents. The dilemmas it contained could be a variety of things, some just trivial, some quite purposeful, but each needed thought and contemplation to solve, perfect for people who had simple uncomplicated lives, in which nothing in particular ever happened.

Along the side wall of the shop were rows of glass bottles, all different colours and sizes, all glinting in the candlelight. The quandaries were fun: the liquid could change to a smoky colour when touched, if it wanted to be chosen, but if you drank it down while still clear, it tasted bitter and made you burp all day.

I remembered one I had chosen some time ago. What do you do if your aunt is coming to stay, the one who knitted you a perfectly silly Christmas jumper in the most daring of colours, which you had let the dog sleep on for some time now? Of course I spent an hour trying to pull the hairs off with sellotape; I was bound to be discovered.

I looked intently at the gentle green eyes of the man behind the counter. 'I have come to change my mind.'

'Ah, of course,' he said, 'let me see.'

He reached down to a large bunch of keys hanging from his belt. The dim light reflected the thin shiny brown stripes of his trousers, as he chose a key and unlocked the panelled door behind him. He ushered me through into a long narrow passageway. There were doorways on each side. The one on my right opened as we approached and a lady came out, with a jaunty greeting to us both. Under her arm she had several travel brochures, all of which looked well-thumbed. That room was the Ponder Room. There were no furnishings, just plain walls, a warm fire and a big comfortable armchair – a quiet place where you could gather your thoughts.

The next room along I had not been in. It was the Deliberating Room. The door was ajar and I could see mirrors around the walls, lots of different seats and a set of scales on a large table. This was a place for weighing up the odds, somewhere to see all sides of a situation. But it was more than this that I needed from Fickleworth's today. I needed help.

The gentleman came to another door. This was the Inconceivable Room. He stopped and opened the door, letting me pass inside before closing the door behind me. There was a huge sofa in the middle of the floor. The seat was just high enough for me to put my hand on, but there was no way I could sit down on it easily. The floor seemed plastic, not sound under me, making me feel dizzy. I leaned with my back against the sofa side and closed my eyes. My insecurities came flooding back, pressing down on my shoulders and quickening my breathing. I must not look backward, I whispered; just think about a good memory, something from my childhood.

There was a seed, a day when something unexpected came. I remember my brother running in, excited and panting to say that he had seen a ginormous lady, with flowing skirts, a soothing, velvet voice and dancing eyes, hanging a poster on a tree. He was waving a flyer; it depicted a huge red and yellow striped tent, with flags flying from the pinnacle and the words 'Grayson's Amazing Illusions' printed across the front. He dropped a small wooden box on the table where my mother was peeling potatoes. She opened it to find frogs hopping out and all over the kitchen!

I giggled in recollection and opened my eyes to wipe a tear from them. The light in the room had softened and changed. One or two pictures of smiling acrobats and prancing horses were hanging on the wall and there was sand beneath my feet. The sofa was still there behind me, the seat up to my chest height, so I climbed onto it and stretched out.

There was a pack of cards on the cushion. I shuffled them several times and lay them down, splayed. I did not want to tempt fate so I swirled them round in a clockwise direction, one, two, three, four, twelve, twenty or so times, until suddenly one fell from my fingers and landed on the floor. Cautiously I peeked over the side and looked at the card. There was just a bird on it, but it was a fantastic bird, with purple and gold feathers and the most amazing curved tail. As I looked up, I saw that the air was filled with tiny birds: blue, darting, mischievous birds, flashing and whirring about. A warm breeze stroked my cheek and palm trees rustled above my head. I felt such an immeasurable glow of pleasure as I stirred from the far-reaches of my mind. I knew I could be settled and happy, if I only changed my mind to it. It was clear I could bumble on doing what I always had done, feeling in my safe zone, comfortable. Or I could try, try something inconceivable. I reached into my bag and found a folded letter, the letterhead showing it was from a flying school. It was an application to become a pilot, a dream I had always had but I'd never been able to conceive of myself actually doing it. Why not give it a try? I climbed down from the sofa and looked back at the room, a busy cluttered room, the walls festooned with pictures.

I opened the door and stepped out again into the passageway. There was a man there, dressed in a businesslike suit, holding a briefcase in one hand. He was fumbling with his free hand along the wall opposite me.

'Are you alright?' I said as I saw him struggling.

'I am looking for the handle,' he muttered sharply, a sense of hopelessness in his tone.

I gently ran my fingers along the wall, calmly, until they closed around the knob. I pushed it open and he stood blinking in the pure white light that issued forth. The Unfathomable Room was one I had never entered before; I pitied the poor man as he looked down the never-ending length of the room, stretching on almost as far as he could see.

'I need to know what to do next,' he said with a longing in his eyes that told me he had reached his wits' end. I smiled warmly as I left him and retraced my steps into the dusty shop.

'Thank you,' I said as I stood in front of the counter. 'I do not know what I would do if you were to retire.'

'Not much chance of that,' Francis Fickleworth said, winking at me as the bell rang again.

The Lone Woman

Caroline Stewart

I felt slightly uncomfortable in the company of all these men. That was strange, as it never normally bothered me, but this was different. I felt like I didn't belong and they knew that. They pushed and jostled to get a better view, grubby hands grasping through the throng of bodies. Some of these men obviously had experience of this sort of thing. They knew what they wanted and they snatched like hungry children. Others were new to it. They gazed around at the beauties on display, mouths wide open in awe. They wandered up and down drinking it all in and not knowing where to start. An hour or so passed by and I couldn't take any more. I had to get out of there. The single-minded obsession of these men was suffocating.

'I'm just going for some air,' I said to my partner and pushed my way through the sweaty crowd to the door. As I got outside I breathed in deeply and vowed that I would never again visit a Model Railway Exhibition.

Nowt To Do

Paula Harrison

What happy days; I wish they would last forever. I enjoy looking after my nephew, he is so easy to care for and entertain, quite happy opening and closing the gate for visitors walking along the old railway path. The visitors are friendly and speak pleasantly to both of us. Some even give him a few pence for his trouble.

Late one afternoon a lone walker appeared at the gate. 'Do you two live here?' he asked. We replied that we did, expecting him to ask about local history or wildlife. He went on to ask, 'What on earth do you find to do in a God-forsaken hole like this? There's nowt to do!' We looked at him in amazement, briefly explaining the beauty of our surroundings and the endless attractions of country life.

John and I walked back home. We played a bit of cricket in our garden that regularly becomes the local pitch in the summer. After tea we turned our attention to damming up the river which runs alongside the garden. John made yet another attempt at teaching me to fish. I think he soon realised he was wasting his time as within minutes I had the line tangled in a tree. 'You are a daft old aunty,' he laughed.

'I know, I have had plenty of practice with you,' I laughed back at him.

After a pleasant evening in his company, I returned John to his parents. 'There's nowt to do here,' he shouted after me, grinning.

*

I glanced through the diary. My morning was to be spent riding. 'Right,' I thought, 'I must get sorted.' I brought the tack out of its store and cleaned everything. The phone rang and a familiar voice asked, 'Can you check out that walk up at Blakey with me tomorrow? It's a good forecast.'

'Yes, I'll be there,' I said.

'How's the summer programme shaping up?' she enquired.

'Nearly finished. I'll bring it on Saturday.'

'Oh, whilst you're there, can you check out that Wolds walk next week?'

'Look, you know there's nowt to do here,' I laughed.

Later that day the schedule for Egton Show arrived. I read through the classes that I like to enter: wine, photographs, flowers and baking. Aware that Danby, Farndale and Lealholm schedules had already arrived, I wandered out to the shed and realised that I'd need to bottle quite a lot of wine for all of these. The process of making wine at home is time-consuming, but a real pleasure, and it is a good discipline to compete in the local shows.

I looked at the photography section of the schedule. I take a lot of photos during the year. How lucky we are to live in such a photogenic area! One of the best times to take photos is during the depths of winter.

I walked down the garden to look at the vegetable patch. It all looked healthy. We're not experts, but we enjoy having a go at vegetable gardening. I thought of the time spent when the tiny seedlings started to grow; regular watering, putting the seedlings in at night, then planting out, followed by more regular watering and netting to keep out the rabbits and birds. Considering there's nowt to do I felt extremely busy.

After the shows, autumn arrives quickly. We pick fruit, prepare it for the freezer or make it into jams and pickles. We store potatoes, beetroot and courgettes. We dead-head flowers, cut back the dying plants and give the grass a final mowing. We sort kindling, chop and split logs and store them ready for the winter.

We take part in village life regularly. We like the evening visits to the Crossing Club for its range of good beers and local involvement, and the leisurely walk to Beck Hole on a Sunday lunchtime for a pleasant drink. We use the library in the old school where there is a varied selection of books. It fills a valuable gap since the mobile library is no longer scheduled to visit Esk Valley. We are members of the newly formed Gardening Group with its visits, talks and contribution to the church and village. At Christmas the church was decorated and Grosmont hosted the Christingle Service. Considering there's nowt to do I always seem to be kept occupied. Christmas and New Year were social occasions with two parties and many other social gatherings.

Winter continues, it snows again. We check the freezer. We make another six loaves of bread and some more soup. We're down to the last jar of marmalade so we make another six.

The phone rings regularly. There is a work day at the Guide's holiday house and campsite in Esk Valley. Help is required for the spring clean. The Trefoil Guild (the group for former Guide leaders) invite me to join them. (Better keep a low profile, they may want a Ranger Guide Unit setting up.) The phone rings again: 'Your application to be a voluntary ranger for the National Park has been processed. Can you be at Danby on Sunday to work alongside the permanent ranger staff. There is a big event at Danby Lodge – we would like you to help please.'

The steam trains start running again between Pickering and Grosmont, adding interest and photographic possibilities.

Winter turns into spring. The tepee parties start again: excellent social evenings under the stars with homemade wine, food and good company. We dig over the vegetable patch, check the compost and plant the seeds for the summer.

The phone rings. It is a request from the village: 'Can Esk Valley be responsible for the cake stall at the Church Fete?'

Another phone call, this time from the Gardening Group. 'Waterloo Gardens are being dug over. Can you help?' And the following day the church is being decorated for Easter. There's the wood to organise for the crosses for Easter Saturday.

Another unexpected task: the chimney caught fire last night. It caused quite a stir with blue lights and firemen. We'll need to blitz the front room now.

So yeah mate, there's nowt to do for you here, but we've got everything: big skies, sunsets, moors, hills, flowers ... We don't have your twenty-four hour bars, concrete jungles or industry. So if ever I come to visit your area, I'd have nowt to do.

Can't Buy Me Love

Josephine Esterling

Little Jenny put her arms around her mother. 'I love you mummy,' she said innocently. One of the woman's arms slowly encircled the child and lay limp about her waist. Somewhere inside her the child begged the woman to look at her, to hold her tight and return the love that she gave so freely. But the woman never looked up from her book.

'I love you,' Jenny said again. This time with a note of urgency in her voice. The woman's arm tightened around the child's waist in response, as though acting love for her daughter. To Jenny it was cold, uncaring and false. She could not understand why her mother did not love her, why she had to continually act out a scene of false sincerity. But to Jenny, any form of love, even this cold love, was better than nothing.

At night Jenny lay unmoving in her bed. Sometimes she would watch the reflected lights of passing cars on the bedroom wall. But mainly she listened.

From the rooms below, muffled voices of her mother and father wafted through the floor. Sometimes they were loud and she could hear every word clearly. That is when the pain in her chest would come. It would be slight at first, like a tiny butterfly battering its delicate wings against her insides. Then it would grow stronger with the voices of her parents until it stabbed at her heart in sharp thin strokes, making her curl up with pain. But Jenny never cried out. Instead she covered her ears with her small hands and cried silent tears into her pillow, all the time wishing her mother and father would stop shouting at each other and love her.

*

Jenny, now seven, stood on the grey concrete path, her eyes shut, arms wide, her finger tips stretching out to the exhilarating void she had spun herself into, until it faded, and reality returned. Again she stepped round and round, one foot following the other, until she was once again dizzy, her body trying to defy gravity as it wobbled and wavered to keep upright, her mind whirling out into space and back again. It felt good, it felt safe. It was wonderful. The more Jenny spun the better she felt. She wondered if that was how it felt to be loved.

'Jenny!'

The child stopped. Her mother called again.

Suddenly Jenny felt sick. Her mother's voice had a note of anger to it. Jenny's heart missed a beat. What had she done, or not done? She could not remember. She felt sick. She was going to be sick.

The mother found the child on the front path with the remains of orange sick dripping down her cotton dress. The rest lay in a pool at the child's feet.

Jenny stood stiff and dumb, watching her mother storm up the path. A tear ran slowly down her face. She braced herself for the blow that would surely come.

Later, Jenny nursed her swollen cheek as she lay in her bed listening. She wanted very much to sleep and to be loved.

*

Jenny watched the child in the garden, spinning round and round. She smiled. 'You'll be sick,' she thought, and put the tea towel down on the drainer and stepped out into the garden. Laughing, Jenny scooped her daughter up into her arms. Together they spun round and round until they were both quite dizzy, and fell onto the grass in a happy, loving, dizzy heap.

The Vestry Door

Tamsyn Naylor

The sun was hidden by heavy dark clouds. Rain started to fall onto the path in large spots as I pushed against the wind to reach shelter. Grotesque figures stared down at me from the roof, waiting to take their fill of life's blood, when the clouds burst. I pushed against the heavy door, forcing a creak from the worn oak timbers, and entered. There was a strange stillness inside, the air damp and musty as I humbly crossed the flagged floor. Opening the vestry door, there was a lull in the roar of the wind outside, which had seemed strangely distant above the lofty roof space. I had been many times before, to tidy and clean the church, but today my senses were heightened by the oncoming storm.

As the first few shafts of sun filtered through the cloudy window pane, my attention was drawn to the glint above the door handle. Pushing the door to, I revealed the relic in full: a magnificent breastplate, retrieved from the battlefield and preserved for over 500 years in this quiet place. As I ran my fingers across it to reveal the marks of the hammer that had beaten it flat, my mind took me back to the day it saw conflict. Reaching for a cloth, one quick rub and the form of the plate began to show itself, dints and delves of damage, which it sustained from the heavy volleys of arrows used in battle and a sharp slash across the shoulder area. Was this caused by a sword? How did the man die? Surely the breastplate would be fierce protection against most weapons, but there must be weak points; maybe he was stabbed through his armpit or an attack from high, through the neck, caused the fatal blow.

Touching the cold steel, I shut my eyes and thought back to the warm heart that once beat below my fingers, a heart that must have been fierce, determined and loyal to his cause. How would you choose which side to take when it came to such a destructive conclusion? Why would you decide to leave the simple way of life that most men must have led, farming and providing, to take up the cause? Did it really matter to the humble classes who sat on the throne, or was honour involved, a man's pride to fight for?

These thoughts ran through my head as I smoothed the cloth along the choir stalls, with the pride of someone getting their horse ready for its ride. The polish was the dubbin on the leather harness; the smoke from a blown-out candle, the breath of the animal as it pulled its head up impatiently; the hoof scraped on the dry earth and a glint of excitement in its eye was the shine from the candlestick as I lifted and replaced it. The bunch of keys that hung from my pocket was the bit he champed on, in his eagerness to run, in anticipation of the chase. The bells rang to the sound of sword-fighting, metal on metal. How terrifying but terrific it must have been to fight on the ground, in the midst of the action. There was no distance-fighting then, no pressing a button or releasing a trigger into an unknown. You were face to face with your enemy and you could not only see and hear them, their strong strained breath, but you could also smell them, smell the sweat and emotion.

The storm had passed over now and sunlight streamed once more, through the stained-glass windows, casting a blood-red hue across the altar steps. It took my gaze to the musty carpet, running along the front of the steps, which had been kicked slightly askew, revealing the smoothly-hewn stone underneath, which had an inscription that I had never noticed before. I rolled the rug back and uncovered the complete stone which read:

'Here lyeth the mortal remains of Edwin Byers
who liveth and dyeth
with a true heart and mind.'

After the battle what would happen to the field? There must have been absolute carnage, with mutilated bodies everywhere. How do you deal with the disposal? Local people must have walked onto the field and picked over the bodies; there would be very few items to identify who these gallant men were and the sight must have been terrible. The breastplate would have been quite a prize to find intact. There must have been a feeling of sadness to keep it, such wasteful loss of life and such brutality. Where were most of them buried? In a ditch somewhere, away from predators?

Local knowledge told me that the church was not on the site at the time of the battle. It was built as a commemoration by the local Lord, as a reminder of the victory so hard won and the lands he gained as a result.

The gargoyles I ventured past were satisfied now they had drunk their fill. The birdsong revived the charged air and the place felt washed clean. A young girl rode past on a flighty cob, rattling the new bit in its mouth as it got used to being tamed. The cob would, no doubt live a long life; the most startled it would feel in its life would be from a pheasant starting up at the crack of a gun. But it would not see warfare, and would not die thrashing around in the sodden field of a battle.

Eulogy

Antony Wootten

'Thomas was ...' I begin. 'He was ...' The church is crowded with mourners: his daughters, his two ex-wives, old friends, locals. Hats bob; the air is still. I'm already struggling to say the words, and I've only just started. I don't know if I'll make it to the end. 'He was my lifelong friend,' I manage. 'My *best* friend.' I am forcing the words from myself, looking out across the congregation of damp eyes and sorrowful smiles. They are united in their love for him, the rogue that he was. As I blunder my way through the eulogy, I find myself glazing over. My own words stir memories which rise like smoke to sting my eyes and cloud my view.

I had met Thomas on my first day at school. That was almost ninety years ago now. The school was a tiny stone building with just one room. It seemed cathedral-sized to me back then; it's an antiques showroom now. He was rough-and-tumble, I was a cry-baby. I don't know why we put up with each other. According to my mother,

Thomas used to steal my toys, and I used to let him. We had a strange relationship, Thomas and I. It was a small village. There weren't many children at all, and we were the only boys our age. We played out together, but, if there had been other boys the same age as us, I wonder if Thomas and I would have bothered with each other.

I'm aware that the church is cold, despite the big heaters whining and wheezing away. I find their noise intrusive and incongruous, but of course I've been coming here all my life, long before the heaters were installed, and now they are as decrepit as I am. I've read a paragraph or two now, and I'm hardly hearing my own words. I thought I'd be able to do it, to keep myself together until the end, and I'm surprised by how much I'm struggling now. And then I get to a sentence which brings the past sharply into my mind. 'He was a war hero ...' That's what I've written, but I know the truth. Only me. He became a war hero, yes, but that wasn't the whole story.

We had the misfortune of being the perfect soldiering age when war broke out. We went off together to fight for our country. Thomas left several broken hearts behind in the village; I left only one, and that was my mother's. I was always the quiet one. Most girls probably didn't even know I existed back then. And I was not tough, not brave. Thomas was. Everyone knew that. I wonder now if my mother ever expected me to return. As it happened, we had a quiet time of it for the first several months of our service, sailing around Africa all the way to the Far East. In fact, I think it was almost six months before we saw any fighting. We were lucky, for that long at least.

But we'd had our fair share of the action by the end of it. It's funny, but we were always together, even though Thomas was a real lad and everyone wanted to get him drunk, or hear him tell a joke or sing a bawdy song, and I was quiet and uncomfortable, never quite sure if people wanted me there or not. In fact, the only time anyone paid me much attention was when Thomas said something disparaging about me, which he did quite a lot, to get a laugh. Yet somehow that put me slightly at my ease, and we stuck together. So, when we were pinned down by enemy fire one day, it was he and I who crawled on our bellies into a bomb crater as the shells and bullets screamed overhead. We rolled to relative safety in the mud, and looked at each other. Neither of us had ever fired our guns in anger by that time, and were both struggling to keep ourselves together. Those two little infants from the village school ... how had we ended up here?

And when a Japanese soldier rolled himself over the crater's lip, also seeking cover, none of us knew what to do. The soldier obviously hadn't known the crater was already occupied, and he practically landed on my head. We all suddenly panicked, and scrambled away from each other, but the Jap was clearly more experienced than us, and had his wits about him. His rifle was pointing straight at us before Thomas and I had even remembered which way round ours went. There was a brief, painful, desperate silence between the three of us as the Jap decided which of us to kill first. Then he pointed his rifle at me and pulled his trigger, but the wet weapon didn't fire. As he pulled back the bolt for his second go, a touch of anguish in his narrow eyes, I fumbled ineffectually with my rifle, which I had ended up partially sitting on, and he pulled his trigger again. Still it didn't fire, but he was so fast! He was on me, shoving my rifle so that I fired it into the mud, and his knees were in my gut and his hand at my throat ... I fought him but he had me pinned. All I could do was struggle and thrash like when Thomas and I used to wrestle at school - he'd always get the better of me, just like the Jap was now. But suddenly the Jap went rigid, then limp. He fell on me, his neck bleeding into my face. I rolled him off me and turned, breathless and shaking, to thank Thomas, but Thomas was just disappearing over the top of the crater's edge, and his rifle was still there where he'd been sitting. He'd panicked, and left me, and a stray bullet had killed the Jap.

We never, ever talked about that, Thomas and I.

But Thomas pulled himself together and became a war hero. One day he dragged our bleeding and shouting sergeant major from the battlefield. Even as the blood pumped from the stump of the major's severed leg, the cantankerous old sod was still roaring motivational disdain at his men, most of whom had already fled. Thomas dragged him backwards through the mud to safety. It was a brave act, and one which Thomas never stopped bragging about. He'd obviously forgotten about the Jap in the crater. And he never mentioned the brave things he saw me do. No. He was the war hero, not me.

Hail on the windows is competing with the rattling heaters now, and some of the congregation are quietly slipping their coats back on. 'He was very well loved ...' I find myself saying. It's true, he was well loved. The fact that this draughty old church is packed to the rafters on a day like today is testament to that. His big, shiny coffin is surrounded by flowers, and no-one seems able to take their eyes off it. How fitting that he should be the centre of attention, even in death. After the war, Thomas was often the centre of attention in the pub, entertaining the old folk and the young ladies with exaggerated tales of his own exploits. Some young ladies, a certain type, were particularly impressed, so much so that they took him to their beds. Then he had more exaggerated tales of his own exploits to tell. I didn't ever really mind that he got all the attention and I was always his straight-man, and sometimes his fall-guy too. He still made jibes about me in front of the girls and the lads he was trying to impress. I'd grown up with that; it didn't hurt or offend me, not in any conscious way at least. In fact, I barely even noticed it. It was my mother who would point it out to me, but we were grown up now, Thomas and I. After the horrors we'd been through together, all I wanted was peace. Besides, we were friends. I knew he was only joking. And by then I had fallen in love with Silvia, and she had fallen for me, so Thomas could do and say what he wanted. I really didn't care.

I hear my own voice droning on: '... popular with the ladies ...' This draws a knowing titter from some members of the congregation, despite their sorrow. Indeed he was popular with the ladies. Very popular. There were some women I'd expected to see right through his act, to see beyond the bravado and jokes, but they didn't; even some of the sharp, clever girls. He could charm anyone.

Even Silvia.

I couldn't believe she could be so blind, but more than that, I couldn't believe he'd betray me like that. How could he? He knew I loved her. And yet, the pain it caused me was more to do with *his* betrayal than *hers*. Thomas and I were friends through circumstance; two totally different people who had played together since our earliest days just because there was no-one else to play with, but I suppose I'd been won over by his charms just like everyone else. I was heartbroken, but in the end, I realised that the thought of losing Thomas was worse than the thought of losing Silvia.

I didn't want to forgive him, but he was like a

brother to me. Besides, we were both still living in the village. Our lives were entangled. I swallowed my pride, and my sorrow, and let him back in.

I look up, for a moment, at some of the faces before me. Many of them are people I know, but very few of them are people I know well. I know them through Thomas. I've met them at his parties and gatherings, or at one of his weddings. They are all wearing that strange expression of both grief and fondness merged together, like heavy rain oddly backlit by evening sun. 'He was a successful politician ...' I remind them. He was. He had the gift of the gab of course. He talked himself onto the local village council, and his career went from there. He was kind enough to give me a job as an office clerk. I think this was sort of his way of saying sorry for Silvia, but looking back I can see it was also a way of keeping me in check. I think, deep down inside, he saw me as some kind of competition. Not that I ever competed with him for jobs, or women, or the respect of our friends and neighbours, but somehow he pitted himself against me, and always came out on top. This was something I only realised in much later years, long, long after the death of my wise old mother who had seen through him right from the start.

I worked for Thomas for many long years. He knew how to throw a great Christmas party, and got himself voted into local government time and time again. A long and illustrious career he had, and I was there with him, at his heels, the whole

Antony Wootten

time. We both retired after three long decades together, during which time he had been married twice, fathered at least six children by at least three different women, and I'd had a lovely marriage of my own. My Margaret. She had seen what Thomas was like. She could see right through him just like my mother had done. The stupid thing was I always found myself defending him to her. She was happy enough to accept him as my friend, but always careful to point it out to me when she felt he had said something cutting, or derogatory. He said such things without even realising it, without meaning it. I never felt there was malice in him. But Margaret would just raise her eyebrows knowingly, as if she didn't believe that I couldn't see it.

It all seems too long ago now. Margaret has gone. My mother went long before she did. And now Thomas has gone too.

There was only one way in which fate was cruel to him; it crippled him with arthritis in his later years. But he'd never given in to it, and I have to say I admired his tenacity. I tried to talk him into getting a stairlift, but he wouldn't hear of it. He was too proud. He wouldn't accept that he could barely walk, let alone get up and down the stairs anymore. Towards the end, I'd pop in several times a day, often bringing him some shopping – there was no way he could get to the shops anymore, and he certainly wasn't going to be seen 'pootling about on one of those dreadful old-people's dodgem cars' as he called them. So he relied on me, and one or two others, to do his shopping, vacuuming, washing ... He was often upstairs when I went round though. I was sure he put himself through that torture before I arrived just so I would see that he was able to get up there. I wasn't fooled. I knew each ascent was a painful, exhausting battle for him. I walk with a stick myself now and I find the stairs hard enough without the curse of arthritis. Once or twice he even conceded to let me help him get back down again. It was awful to see how such an agile, lively man had been twisted and withered by this disease. Still, we both agreed, there were worse things in the world. He still had his marbles, and his memories.

But that was his only suffering. He'd lived a charmed life. His daughters loved him, despite his regular dalliances. Even his ex-wives still seemed pretty well-disposed towards him. He was fondly remembered by the community for his political work and his wonderful parties. Sometimes, I wondered what he'd done to deserve all that. I'm not a bitter man, but sometimes it just didn't feel right. That's what my mother would have thought. That's what my Margaret would have thought too.

The other day, I was upstairs in his study. I'd delivered his shopping, vacuumed round a bit, and made him some dinner. He never thanked me. He seemed to feel I owed him this, as payment for his friendship, and perhaps for the employment he'd given me in the past. I was his carer now, though I was suffering the slings and arrows of old age myself too. And ... And ... I hadn't mentioned to him my recent diagnosis. Somehow, I imagined he'd think it was right that I should die before him. He was the better man after all. He had always been more important. I'd always been his minion.

It was my diagnosis which changed me. I am dying. I can't complain. I'm into my nineties. I've had decades more good living than many people get. But still, why should he live longer than me?

I look at the congregation before me. They are all here for him. He really was loved. I wonder how many there will be at my funeral. Some of these people probably didn't even know who I was until today. I have no children, no wife, no fond ex-wives. I haven't done wonderful things for the community. I won't be remembered as a war hero.

But at least I am still here. That is one thing I have over him.

I've stopped reading the eulogy and find myself just staring across the church at nothing in particular. I am remembering how that evening with Thomas ended. We'd chatted over whisky and chess in his upstairs study. I'd offered to help him to the bathroom but he'd refused. I bade him goodbye then, and left him sitting there.

At the top of the stairs was a radiator, and on the radiator, a large, thick towel. I'd put it there myself earlier on after emptying the washing machine for him. I leant on the radiator for extra support as I made my way down the first couple of steps to where the stairs turned a corner. As I did so, I dislodged the towel. I hadn't meant to of course, but as I was about to pick it back up, a thought crossed my mind.

A minute or two later I was at the foot of the stairs, looking up at the fuse box in the hall. It was one of those nice modern ones with trip-switches rather than fuses. It was me who'd arranged for the electrician to come and fit it; the old one had been an accident waiting to happen.

It seems so out of character now, but years and years and years of something I couldn't quite explain had built up inside me without me even knowing it. And I am dying.

I tripped the master switch off and all the lights went out. And I left, almost before I'd heard Thomas calling out to ask why he'd been plunged into darkness.

I made my way home, and I slept very peacefully that night.

In the morning, I let myself into Thomas's house, as I so often did. He was lying at the bottom of the stairs, lifeless. His feet were still partly tangled up in the towel I'd left at the top of the stairs. I popped the master switch back on and the lights sprang needlessly into life. I looked down at him, and felt nothing, although he had been kind to me sometimes; he had been my friend.

I hadn't known for sure that my actions would kill him, but I knew that was what I'd hoped. Now

I would die too, slowly, painfully, but at least I wouldn't be leaving him behind to gloat.

I can't finish the eulogy. After a few long moments of my silence, someone steps up and gently guides me back to my seat. Through my fog of memories and tears I can't even tell who it is. Several people try to soothe me with gentle words, and slowly, like the way a steam engine comes to life, a round of applause begins.

Forgotten

Melanie Allanson

Betty looked out of her second floor window and pondered aloud with a wry smile to the unknown audience, 'So if I jumped? What would they all do, eh?' Her children and grandchildren knew that Nan would always see them right. Lost your priceless car due to defaulting on the payments? Nanny will soon have paid off the loan or bought you a new one to replace it. Dropped out of college? Taken too many drugs to see straight anymore? Nanny will sort it out, paying off debts, sorting you out with a drugs counsellor and getting you back on your feet again. Husband's had an affair? Phone Nanny Bets, she'll be sure to have some sound advice, and a handout if you're lucky. Well, Nanny Betty was sick and tired of people taking her for granted. What use was Nanny without any money?

She had finally run out of her husband Arthur's hard-earned trust money and his shares and she had spent the lot on her family. Now she had no more to give them.

She sat down heavily on the chair looking out of the window. Selfish lot, they needed to learn to stand on their own feet and not rely on her. She felt a pang of guilt as she knew that since the love of her life, Arthur, had died she had been very lonely and glad to bail them all out and make their lives easier. She hadn't been clued up enough with the shares; how could she have known that they could go down in value as well as up? Now it was nearly all gone. The flat would have to be sold and she would have to ask the council for somewhere to live, which would be so humiliating after being able to have whatever she'd wanted for all these years.

She sniffed as tears rolled down her wizened face and she realised that she was an old fool and nobody really would care if she were gone. Arthur had been so careful with his money and although generous, had always kept some for a rainy day; he would wink at her when he said this. He had bought their flat with a large deposit which he had been saving up for ever since he'd first laid eyes on Betty, aged ten! She used to laugh at the earnest young man three years her junior who wanted to carry her books and packed-lunch for her. Well, at first she had laughed and ribbed him with her friends, but as the years rolled on, she thought how kind and thoughtful he was, not like the other boys who were too busy striking conquests and rushing through her class mates like they were on fire and they were definitely just out for a bit of fun. No, Arthur was kind, gentle, considerate and over the years had become more and more besotted with Betty.

What she did not realise at that time was that Arthur had decided she was the one for him, and he was going to woo her for as long as it took. He saved all of his pocket money and birthday money every time in a savings account. Then he had left school and started working at the local supermarket and again he banked most of his wages for a house for his wife to be. Over the years he continued to love Betty and even though she had a few boyfriends, he knew she would turn to him when it all went wrong. There were other girls who tried to get him to take them out but he would politely refuse and tell them that there was only one lady for him and he wouldn't want to waste their time. The girls used to look at Betty with envy that she had a man who was so besotted with her, and yet she seemed unaware.

Then, one day Arthur found her outside his house sobbing and unable to talk. He took her to a cafe, bought her a strong tea and listened to her tale of woe. It involved a boy called Tommy going off with her best friend, and not only that but he had been two-timing her for weeks. Whilst she dried her eyes he looked at her with a radiant smile and asked her out. She said yes and that was it, Betty never wanted for anything. Arthur made it his mission to provide anything she wanted.

Soon they were married and living in a house bought with his savings and a bank loan. They had three children and had many happy years together. Then five years ago he had become ill, losing weight and looking a ghastly yellow colour and the doctors had sat Betty down and told her that her lovely Arthur was going to die, and the following year they were right. So she had surrounded herself with her children and grandchildren and made sure nobody ever had to struggle, but it seemed she had spoiled them all and no-one visited unless they were in trouble.

Betty noted that it was growing dark outside, but she could see some figures coming through the opening in the hedge to her flats. She watched the small gathering wind their way around the grounds to the entrance to her block of flats. Then she turned away from the window. Well, someone was going to get some visitors. 'Lucky them,' she said under her breath and dragged heavy feet into her kitchen to make a cup of tea. She remembered her mum's words, how things could always seem better with a nice cup of tea.

Minutes later she heard a knock on her door and lots of noise from behind it. The voices of her family, all her loved ones that she had helped over the years. She pulled the door open and couldn't help feeling cross with them all, despite a small part of her feeling happy to see them. They would have to convince her that they weren't after money or something else.

It then dawned on her that her family all looked concerned. They were loaded down with plates of food and thermos flasks and a picnic basket. She ushered them into her tiny flat. As she did so she received several hugs from her grandchildren. 'Nanny, we've been so worried about you. We keep inviting you over but you never return our calls. We've texted and emailed but you don't reply, so we've come to see you and then you are coming to stay with our Mark and Sally and then Trisha and Paul!' She had to smile as she didn't know how to work the mobile phone they had given her a few weeks ago and she certainly couldn't email. Then she realised that the phone had rung a lot lately but she had been so wrapped up in her own thoughts that she had assumed it was salesmen and had not bothered to answer. She did vaguely remember her son, Derek, telling her about the answer-phone and how to use it, but she hadn't taken much notice. She'd not thought there was any point, she no longer had the energy to support everyone. Perhaps, she now realised, she'd been making excuses. She wasn't daft. If she was to honest with herself, she knew she could have learned to use the answer-phone and her mobile, but, deep inside, she just hadn't wanted to.

Now, seeing her family gathered around her, she felt her spirits lift. They did care, and now it was time to let them look after her.

The Dead Ringer

Paul Wootten

Reverend Martin Coates sighed contentedly. Another successful Thursday evening was reaching its end. He could hear the sounds of Mrs Jarvis as she pottered about in the church swishing a duster here and there. She was new to the parish and the post of church cleaner and it amused him just how fastidious she was; every hymn book in its place; every hassock just so.

The vacuum cleaner started up again. How absurd it sounded echoing in the high vault of these ancient stones which rang only a short while before with the last reverberations of the great bells. He loved Thursday evenings: choir practice followed by bell-ringing with just a few friends. They had all gone now and in a few minutes Mrs Jarvis would finish and he could go home to his wife.

The mist of late April dusk was descending over the churchyard, making everything grey. These Norfolk flat-lands suffered the brisk northeasterlies most of the time, but when the wind dropped, the sea mist would roll in. Martin glanced out through the vestry window. This was his church, and how well the parish had flourished under him: the churchyard so neat and trim; he had seen to that: no more nettle patches or overgrown hiding places for the boys to play in. This was his churchyard.

Something made him stay at the window longer than the original cursory glance would have allowed. Was there someone sitting on a tombstone under the hawthorn? He could not be sure. With his pocket handkerchief he wiped the diamond of glass inside the black lines of lead. Had he been mistaken? There was no-one there now and yet he was sure he had seen the figure of a young woman perched on the stone, her head on one side, looking at the church; her long, blonde hair splashed carelessly around her shoulders. 'Emma Gill ...!' His voice had framed the words before he could stop it. He loathed talking to himself but seemed to be doing more of it recently. He knew it was ridiculous because, just a year ago, he had buried Emma Gill close by that hawthorn. He remembered how the twisted branches, later in the year, had sprinkled the grave with its snowy blossom, the only confetti she was ever to call her own.

She had been one of his bell-ringers, and so pretty that many hearts were broken when they found her amongst the reeds at the bottom of the river. He peered hard through the glass but only the mist moved around the grave-stones. There was no-one there.

The vacuum cleaner had stopped. He went through into the church. The lights were all out, Mrs Jarvis had gone. He locked the vestry door and headed for home. He could not help pausing however to look at the stone by the hawthorn tree as he passed:

'In loving memory of
Emma Gill
called before her time.
1968 – 1990'
*

'James, leave your brother alone! You know he won't sleep if you fill his head with nonsense like that.'

'But it isn't nonsense, Mum. I did see her, honest!'

Mrs Caton often had problems getting the boys to bed. Since the death of her husband she had given James more responsibility than she should have done. She knew it, but the two boys had been all she had to comfort her during those bleak months.

'Look Mum! After Scouts we always go home past the church, and we sometimes play 'it' down by the wall. We've found some super new hiding places since they cut the grass. Then suddenly,' he dropped his voice to an affected whisper, 'everything went cold and we saw this figure, all in white, sitting on a grave-stone. It was that girl who drowned last year. I know it was.'

His brother's mouth dropped open, his wide, unwavering eyes fixed upon James' face. James noticed with satisfaction. 'We decided to creep up on her,' he continued. 'We slid into the shadows and crept from grave-stone to grave-stone. But when we'd got there she'd gone! It was a ghost alright!'

'Well, that's quite enough of that. Go on both of you, off to bed. It's alright, Gary, there are no such things as ghosts.'

Gary's mouth closed with a jerk.

*

Gary was not the only one to sleep badly that night. Mrs Caton lay awake for a long time remembering how shaken they had all been by the death of Emma Gill. 'Funny', she thought, 'that James should bring this up now. It must be almost a year ago that she died.'

Everyone had liked Emma and the years away at the University had only helped this spring bud to bloom into maturity. What a waste it had been of one filled with such promise.

The next morning she mentioned the story in the village shop, as Mrs Kirby, the shop keeper, lurked behind the glass and stainless steel bacon-slicer on the counter and traded more than merchandise in the heady atmosphere of warm bread and newspapers.

'Oh, these churchyards are all haunted you

know. A pound and a half of bacon was it?'

'Yes please, and a pound of that nice Cheddar. How is Mrs Gill these days? I haven't seen her for so long.'

'Well, no, she keeps much to herself now, but she's okay. This piece? I'll bet she wishes now that she had kept her on a tighter rein. All those boys, well I ask you! Not to speak ill of the dead, but if she had spent more time helping her mum and less running after the boys she would still be here today.'

'But,' Mrs Caton interrupted, 'her mother was terribly proud of her, and I believe she was very clever, going to the university and all.'

'Ah yes, but clever at making people do what she wanted, I'm afraid. You should have seen her hanging around here when she was younger. Had all the boys drooling over her, she did, and played them off against each other mercilessly.'

'I had no idea.'

'Well, I tell you! You learn a few things in a job like this. Did you say a dozen eggs?'

Mrs Caton breathed deeply in the fresh air outside the shop and wondered.

*

Later that morning, back in the rumour-ridden atmosphere of butter pats, cheese rind and brown, curled bacon, Mrs Kirby watched Mr Thompson as he picked at the milk bottles in the cold cabinet. Would he choose skimmed today? She watched with mild interest as he turned to place two bottles on the counter.

'Special occasion is it?' she asked. 'Here, you remember Emma Gill don't you? Well, Mrs Caton says that her ghost was seen walking the graveyard yesterday. What do you think of that?'

Mr Thompson did not think much of it at all, but would like half a pound of sausages and a packet of tea. 'You don't get ghosts when someone just falls off a bridge and drowns,' he muttered. 'You have to have something unnatural for that like murder or suicide. No! Typhoo please.' And he left her to the blowfly-buzzing silence of the shop where spectres rose and fell like shadows among the jars of pickle and the faded packets of home-perm.

'A fruit loaf you said, Mrs Greaves? Mr Thompson thinks there was something funny about the death of Emma Gill. You remember, last year, the pretty thing they found in the river. Well, her ghost was seen in the grave-yard yesterday. He thinks she might have committed suicide.'

'They all said it was an accident. But who knows what goes on in a young girl's mind. I'll tell you what I think Mrs Kirby ... Ooh! I'll have a piece of that fruit cake please.' Then, lowering her voice as if to protect the packets of biscuits from this revelation, continued. 'I used to ring the bells on Thursdays and so did she. Always stayed behind afterwards, she did, to help the vicar clear up, she said. Well, we all knew what that meant! Oh! Good afternoon, Mrs Coates,' as the small brass bell that hung beside the door rang to interrupt their conversation and send the ghosts of past gossips scurrying away to hide beside the stack of brooms in the corner, or to creep back into Mrs Kirby's apron pocket.

*

Reverend Martin Coates sat in the vestry. It had been a bad week. He had felt on edge somehow. He had not seen the girl on the gravestone again even though he had taken time each day to look, chastising himself continuously for his own foolishness. This Thursday evening had not been as pleasant as usual either. He seemed unable to concentrate during hymn practice and felt that some of the choir had noticed his vagueness and were talking furtively about him. Once or twice he had caught the odd look that left him outside the conversation, wondering. Mrs Jarvis, who only came once a week, arrived late, interrupting the bell-ringing to ask for the keys to the cleaning cupboard. He had to go with her to get them from his coat in the vestry. When he returned, the conversation, which had been in full vigour as he approached the ringing-chamber, ceased unnaturally as he entered. Were they criticizing him? For the first time for a long while he felt distinctly uncomfortable.

They had all gone now and he sat thoughtfully in the vestry listening to that infuriating vacuum cleaner rising and falling like a choir of the dead. Tonight of all nights Mrs Jarvis had to be late. All he wanted to do was to get home. He glanced out at the evening.

A fine rain had been falling for most of the day and now, just as the light was going, the sky had cleared to cast a mellow glow on trees and gravestones. His breath caught in his throat. There beneath the thorn tree was the hazy figure of a girl. There was no doubt about it ... It was the same girl as last Thursday, sitting just as she had sat then, her head on one side, watching the church. Oh how he remembered the way that she had looked at him, with those big eyes, her head slightly on one side, on those many evenings, after bell practice, when she had stayed behind to help him clear up. How grown up she had become after the university. Bursting into his mind like flash-bulbs came the images of that last time when she had cornered him beside the bookcase. The smell of her wafted back to him; the fullness of her flesh; the warmth. How he had wanted her. How she had played with him. She knew how to move her body to tease and tantalize, and he knew that he must not touch. But how he had wanted to. The sins he had committed in his mind were haunting him now. He moved over to the window, drawn by this phantom shape. The light had nearly gone and a mist lay upon the path. As he watched, she waved to him and slid off the stone and onto the carpet of swirling silver. Her feet, now trapped in its web, her body as still as a manikin, she glided towards the window. He could hear his heart thump like the deepest bell in his belfry, fit to burst his head. Closer she came. He backed away from the window and felt the desk bite into him, holding him there. His tongue stuck to the roof of his mouth. The handle on the vestry door turned slowly and she was standing before him.

'Hello vicar! I don't think we've met. I'm Dianne Jarvis. Could you tell me mum I can't wait any longer tonight and I'll see her at home? ... Are you alright?'

Reverend Martin Coates had slid quietly to the floor and was now, temporarily at least, communing with other spirits in his ancient churchyard.

His Eyes Opened

Ray Stewart

His eyes opened. The white ceiling looked back at him ... Where was he? He had been walking ... walking ... yes, but to where? He had been on his way to work? No, he had been on his way back home. Home ... to whom? From where? The work had been dirty, he remembered that much. He lifted his hands, but they were clean.

How long had he been lying here? He heard voices outside, distant mumbling voices that did not sound familiar ... voices ... Who had said the fond farewells to him as he went to work that morning? It was that morning that he had gone to work ... wasn't it?

He closed his eyes and the darkness enabled him to see more clearly. He was walking along the old wagon-way. It was all so familiar. He felt tired, well you would do after a twelve hour shift at the Dolly. The Dolly ... That's where he had spent his last twelve hours, hewing coal and swallowing coal dust. He heard a whistle from the other side of the

88

hedge as the coal wagons, carrying the fruits of his labours, were hauled towards the town by a panting black engine. Hannah would have his tea ready when he returned. The bairns would be playing outside the front door. It was much better in the summer when there were still a few hours of daylight when he returned from work. How different in the winter when he left home early in the morning in the darkness, worked for twelve hours in the darkness and then returned home in the darkness.

He opened his eyes to rid himself of the darkness. He looked again at the ceiling. He turned his head slowly to survey his situation and his neck ached. It must have been a heavy shift, he usually didn't suffer from aches and pains. He was still a young man. Closing his eyes he remembered that the Dolly had been his second pit. He had started as a putter at the Peggy when he was fourteen. He had worked at that for about four years, building up his stamina and insensitivity to the pain before he progressed to the coal face as a hewer. He had met Hannah about the same time on a Sunday outing organised by the Chapel. They had started walking-out and it was not long before they were being married in the same chapel, and only seven months later that young Tom was being christened. It wouldn't be long before Tom would be going along with him on *his* first shift. Tom's life was mapped out for him, but his sister Margaret's was yet an open book. The teacher at the village school had told them that she was clever, but as a miner's daughter what doors would be opened for her?

He heard a voice ... He thought that the voice was talking about him ... He opened his eyes again and saw a man he did not know. He was young, tall and he wore a white coat. He was talking to a nurse ... Well, he thought it was a nurse but the white clad figure was wearing trousers ... He looked at the figure and yes, the shape was that of a woman. They were saying that he was stable and the police would be coming soon to talk to him.

He wondered why the police would want to talk to him. He had never crossed the boundaries of the law, apart from the odd poached rabbit.

He closed his eyes again to greet familiarity. He thought about popping into the Three Horseshoes for a quick pint before his tea but walked on realising that one pint would lead to three. It was a fine night and he contemplated an hour on the allotment after his tea. He had a fine crop of taties and carrots this year, and Hannah would soon be making good use of them in the kitchen. He began to ache again and he opened his eyes. The room was stark and clinical. The voices continued a little way off and he was alone. A sudden thirst came over him. Looking around the room he saw a tap over a sink and he moved to fill the empty glass that was beside his bed with some water. He slipped out from beneath the sheet and, taking the glass, he moved unsteadily towards the sink.

Filling the glass he raised it to his lips and, looking into the mirror, he saw a man he did not know.

*

Jenny quietly opened the door and peeped inside. The old man was asleep. She was pleased about that. He had endured a couple of disturbed days since he had been found wandering about on the new Wagonway Industrial Estate. At first no-one had known who he was, as he had carried no identification with him. Gradually, with the assistance of the police, information had been pieced together and a picture of old Jacob had emerged.

There was actually a tenuous connection between Jacob and Jenny. When his daughter had turned up to visit him, she had been recognised by Jenny as her teacher from junior school.

Mrs Elliot had recently retired as Headteacher of St Wilfrid's Junior School, and had recognised Jenny on entering the hospital. They had spent some time that evening reminiscing over people and events from Jenny's schooldays, making Jenny's connection with Jacob slightly more personal than professional. She had taken it upon herself to look in on him whenever she had a moment free from her busy work schedule.

Jacob's wife had died some ten years earlier. His son had been lost in the great waste of 1917 and apparently he had never recovered from this loss.

Jenny was due a break and went to the cafeteria

for a cup of coffee and a bun. She wondered about the confusion that had brought Jacob here under her care, and considered her own confusion.

She had a steady boyfriend, Les, whom she had been with for the best part of three years. He had asked her to marry him but she was not sure, and had remained non-committal. There had been a humdinger of a row a couple of months ago about this and he had stormed off into the night.

It was the night of the party ... *that* party. She had been angry, hurt and uncertain about where she was going. She'd had far too much to drink that night and was certainly not thinking straight.

Then *he* had walked in. He was younger than her, but he was tall and good looking. He made her laugh, which along with the alcohol had helped her to forget the trauma of the earlier argument. She tried to remember the finer details of that evening ... He had not tried to chat her up but at one point during the night they had wandered upstairs and finding an empty room they found themselves in each other's arms kissing passionately. Things had gone further than expected but as they held each other closely she forgot about the argument, and Les ... For a few frantic moments he had ceased to exist.

It had been good, but when she woke up the following morning she was filled with guilt, remorse and a wish that there had been no argument. With no argument, and Les not storming off, *he* would have taken her to the party.

She had dressed and had an unsatisfying breakfast when there was a knock on her door. It was Les of course, remorseful about the previous night's argument and it was not long before they tumbled into bed as a natural conclusion to the reconciliation.

As she looked into her coffee she considered this. She still wasn't sure about a long-term relationship with Les. He was too volatile, and likely to storm off at the slightest provocation.

But things were different now. She now had a secret. She was now two months late and for once, as a medical professional she didn't know what to do.

With time creeping on she returned to the ward after her brief escape from professional responsibilities, and lost herself in the familiarity of her daily routine. It was an uneventful day and as her shift finished, she was uncertain as to whether or not she was pleased to be going home, as she would now have time to contemplate her predicament which had been forgotten during the activity of the day. Before she left she looked in to see old Jacob. Margaret was sitting beside him holding his hand. He was quite agitated and was obviously excited about something. Margaret turned and smiled towards Jenny. 'He's a bit excited. I've just told him that his grandson Bobby is popping in to see him tomorrow night. He's doing very well for himself at school. He's got his A-Levels to do in a couple of months so he's been a bit too tied up to come and see him.' She told Jenny all about the close relationship between Jacob and his grandson: how they had virtually lived up on the allotment when Bobby was younger; how the old man had made him a model boat and took him to sail it on the pond in the park; how Bobby, after a row at home, had run away to 'live' with his granddad. Jenny wondered at the simplicities of the ties between the old man and Bobby and compared it to the complexities of her own life.

She went home and, closing the door behind her, decided to lock herself away from the world.. at least for this evening. She soaked herself in the bath and found some temporary comfort in the enveloping warmth. As she lay in the warm water she dozed and drifted away from her cares. The water cooled a little and she revived, reluctantly stepping out and wrapping herself in a warm towel. The phone rang nearby, and she let it ring, preserving the feeling of isolation that she craved. It was probably her mum, or perhaps Les, but at the moment she did not want to talk to anyone.

She spent the evening in an armchair, watching the television but seeing nothing as thoughts and emotions tumbled through her head. She fell into bed after midnight and slept fitfully as the rain lashed against her window.

Jacob slept well. He drifted in and out of a past existence which was infinitely preferable to his present condition. He looked out of the window as the dawn broke with the growing light gradually painting in the features beyond the hospital grounds. Someone brought him his breakfast and he ate well.

Jenny picked at her toast, but with no appetite most of it found its way into the waste bin. She had a wash and put on her uniform for another day at the hospital.

*

Jacob was livelier today than he had been since he had found his way into this small world within the larger world, in which he had lost his way. Today his favourite grandson was coming to see him and his consciousness of reality was sharper than for many a week. The hours passed unnoticed by Jacob, but for Jenny the time dragged. She popped in to see him to administer his medication and he babbled away about his teatime visitor. He was going to be the 'genius' of the family. He was going to outdo his headmistress-mother and nothing in the world was going to stop him.

She stayed with him to ensure that he made a good attempt at his hospital lunch before retreating to the cafeteria to go through the motions of normality by playing with a plate of lasagne. Around her, colleagues and the odd friend gossiped and laughed with the 'gallows' humour associated with those who dealt with the sick and dying, but Jenny heard nothing.

The routine of the afternoon whittled away at the hours and soon she would reach the end of her shift, when she could retreat into her cocoon of isolation. The clock finally reached four and she signed off, and, putting on her coat, prepared herself for the journey home. As she left the locker room she decided to say goodnight to Jacob and headed in the direction of his room. She looked through the open door and, seeing a crowd of visitors around his bed, turned to slip away. But she was too late. Jacob had spotted her and waved for her to enter. 'This is our Jenny' he said. 'She's the one who looks after me when you lot are not here'. The heads turned to look at her and there looking back at her, dressed in his sixth form uniform was the face of the young tall stranger.

Look at Me Now

Paula Harrison

Mel arrived in the classroom a few minutes before her lesson. Though it was her last day, the classroom showed evidence of on-going projects. The art and crafts area had completed models, colourful batik and printing work. There was something from every child, not just that of the favoured few who consistently produced good work.

She'd been at the school for most of her career. Mel looked out of the window. Nothing had changed much over the decades: the timber yards, the docks, and the high wall of the prison. The kid's lives were mapped out for them in this depressed inner city area. Mel hoped that down the years her pupils would remember her with some affection and as a teacher who really cared about them. She hoped she had given them some preparation for the harsh world outside.

Mel was ready for retirement. Her thoughts wandered for a while. She looked at her drab

97

clothes and old shoes. She felt frumpy compared with the younger members of staff. Mel lived in a neat little terraced house not far from the school. She walked to school and was well known in the community for her work with the homeless and Narcotics Anonymous. Her former pupils often spoke to her as she went about her daily life.

Mel thought about her own family. They had just thrown her away; poking fun when she told them she wanted to go to college. She left those memories behind but thought about her own troubled teenage years. She could have gone down the road of alcohol and drugs. The school she attended recognised her skills and helped her to apply for a place at college. College had been the making of her, helping to leave behind the memories of a dysfunctional family that had eroded every bit of confidence she had. Sometimes Mel felt she hadn't fully recovered from the emotional, cruel battering, and the harsh uncompromising, dictatorial discipline which always appeared to place her in the wrong, when on many occasions she was right. It was often commented that Mel was kind, caring and thoughtful. She still couldn't deal with praise after endless vindictive criticism in her early years.

Those who took the time to get to know Mel discovered that she had a dry sense of humour, a no-nonsense approach to her work and that she didn't suffer fools. Her family chose not to recognise her many skills and attributes, not only in her job, but in her many outside interests as well. Mel gave of herself in everything she did. With a wide circle of friends, she was well respected and called on by others in times of difficulty.

The peace was suddenly shattered by a mixed class of fifteen-year-old children appearing as an unruly, threatening mob. 'Quiet.' Mel didn't shout but used an authoritative voice. 'In, sit down. Right, bring your chairs round me,' she said. The class looked bemused. There was a scuffling of chairs, feet, pushing, and shoving. 'Harry, you sit here and shut that music off.' Sulkily he put his music away.

'Miss, what do we have to sit here for?' asked one of the children, as others addressed each other with remarks such as:

'You only want to sit at the back so we can read those mags your lad got us.'

'Shut up, Duck Head.'

Turning to Mel, a boy said, 'It's your last day today, Miss, isn't it?'

'Yes, Mike, it is.'

'Will our new teacher be old like you?'

'I don't know who has been appointed yet, Mike.'

'Will they give us a party at Christmas like you did? If they don't will you come and do it? Or will you come if they do?'

'Yes to both requests, Mike.'

'Miss, you taught my Dad.'

'Yes, I remember him well.'

'He said you came to see him at that Detention Centre place. He thought all the staff were tossers. He said when they saw you were in the hall he thought, 'Oh Christ, I'm for it now.' Dad said you were alright with him when he came back to school. He said some staff were right twats with him 'cos he'd been in the nick.' Some of the other children joined in the conversation:

'Miss, my mam was fifteen when she had me. She said I have to get a career and have a better life than 'er.'

'Jenny, your mam has a point.'

'Miss, can I go out for a moment?'

'Why, Emily?'

'Miss, I just have to.'

'Go on then, be quick.'

Jenny continued, 'Miss, me mam's kicked me dad out. She said he was a lazy fat bastard who did nowt and left it all to her. She loves us lot but says we're bloody hard work. Miss, I help me mam with the kids.'

'Miss, do you want to leave?' interrupted David.

Mel was thoughtful. 'The best part of my job has been working with you kids. That's why I came into the job all those years ago. Things change, things move forward, nothing stays the same.'

'Miss, what will you do?'

'One of the reasons that I'm retiring is the fact that I have so much to do. I like my work and activities in the community. I like my holidays and friends.'

Emily returned. 'Miss, you have to go to the front hall.'

Mel hadn't realised what was about to happen. 'But I'm about to teach a lesson!'

'Oh Miss, just come on. Come on, just go.'

Mel was escorted out of the class into the front hall. She was overwhelmed. Staff, children, parents, former pupils, former staff were all present.

'Miss, did you know anything about our surprise party for you?'

Mel could hardly speak. 'Jenny, I had no idea. I know that there is a meal tomorrow night, but this is just fantastic.'

Former pupils queued up to speak to Mel.

'Hi, Miss.' Mel looked twice at the six-foot-six man.

'Jim, it's you!'

'Miss, I'm a car mechanic now. I went to College and passed all my exams. The College said you gave me a good report. Thanks, Miss, I might not have done it without you.'

'David, you don't alter. Art College. Your work was amazing.'

'Miss, I'm a photographer now. I've got an exhibition in town.'

'David, I shall be down to see it.'

'Miss, here's your invite. I'll take you round it all.'

'Matthew, now you've a story.'

'Miss, that trouble I got into with handling stolen stuff. I got put away for it. When the cops raided our house, it was all in our loft. It was a blessing in disguise that I was in the nick 'cos that gang got into armed and violent stuff while I was inside. They're inside for twenty years 'cos somebody got killed. I didn't like life inside.'

'Matthew, you weren't a bad lad.'

'Don't faint, Miss, I got a food hygiene certificate inside. I've taken on that little cafe round the corner. There's a grotty little flat above it but we're getting it sorted.'

'Who's 'we'?' asked Mel.

'I've got a lass now. She's sound and works in the cafe. Me and her are just right. She had a lad before me who used to knock her about. I don't live like that. Me dad knocked me mam about when he'd had a few. Me mam's got a new feller now. He's round there now doing some work for us. Miss, her family don't like me 'cos I've been inside.'

'Matthew, I know you. Put the past behind you. You're going in the right direction.'

'Miss, you know everything. Miss, come in to our cafe and I'll show you round.'

Many children just wished Mel a happy retirement. They knew just how much they were going to miss her.

Someone in the corner caught Mel's attention. She wandered over. Mandy Watson, the shy little teenager who wouldn't leave the classroom because she was afraid of the noise in the playground, the shouting of the other children and young adults. At an early age Mandy had become a self harmer. Her parents showed her no compassion. She was just a fool in their eyes.

'Mandy,' said Mel with compassion. 'What are you doing now?'

'Miss, I'm older now. I'm still with the same family even though I'm twenty three. You wrote that report for the social worker, didn't you, Miss?'

'Well, I thought it best that you stayed at the same school.'

'I didn't want to move schools. I never see me mam and dad now. I might as well have never existed. I still need help but my new family help me with all that.'

Mandy saw Mel looking at scars on her wrists. 'I don't do that anymore now, I feel a bit better about myself. I help at a nursery. The staff know about my background and I like the kids. Miss, can I see you again 'cos you helped me all those years ago?'

'That would be lovely, Mandy.'

Mel recognised another former pupil. 'James.'

'Miss, I bet you read about me in the paper. I wasn't driving that car you know, it was John Scrayton. He said he'd torch my pigeon loft if I didn't cowtow to him. It was him that sprayed all that paint on the school wall.' Mel listened to James's story. He wasn't going anywhere in life.

A gentleman in a smart suit was the next person

to speak to Mel. She couldn't place him.

'Mel, you taught me thirty-five years ago. I'm visiting for the weekend, I'd heard about your party and wanted to come.'

'Andrew,' she said.

'I'm a barrister in London now, very different from my early upbringing in the docklands of Hull. Thanks, Mel for believing in me when I didn't always believe in myself. There's someone else here to talk to you, it's Dr McNeil. He's a senior consultant now in Cambridge.'

'Dr Steven McNeil,' Mel said out loud. 'You'll have many letters after your name, the little lad who wanted to be a doctor, the little lad who lived by the dockside in a tiny terrace with eight siblings and no dad at home. Dr Steven McNeil, you made it.'

'Mel, I'm home for a while, get your diary out and come and see us all.'

Several hours had passed in what felt like minutes. Some began to drift off to their various homes. Mel still had many former colleagues who wished to speak to her: colleagues who had been promoted, some to become head teachers and many who, in their early days, had asked Mel for guidance and advice.

Ian Wilson, now head at a local school, asked Mel why she hadn't applied for promotion.

'What did I want to be out of the classroom for?' she replied. 'I like teaching and I like these young adults, life is hard for them. I just liked to help them on their way.'

Ian thought, 'I wish you were at my school, Mel. I wish you were my deputy head rather than the prat I've got now.'

Mick, the head at Mel's school, had a soft spot for her. Soon after he'd taken the post, she'd walked past his office, and found him head in hands. 'Not what you expected, Mick?' Mel said in her usual quiet, calm way. Mick had arrived from an affluent grammar school in Cornwall and expected great things. 'Mick, look out of those windows at the docks, railway, prison, timber yards. We're not great achievers here, success is marked not by academic achievement but by those you keep off drugs and keep out of prison; you just need to give a bit of support to help people get through life.'

Mick was a good head reassessing his priorities. He'd been in post for ten years. He came over to Mel. 'Enjoying it all?' Mel was too overwhelmed to speak. 'Mel, do you remember that school inspector? What did you say to him? He was very red-faced and flustered when he came into my office.' Sometimes, Mick felt like a pupil in Mel's presence.

'Mick, he said I was old fashioned, not done enough in-service training and my classroom didn't show modern trends of teaching. I was doing a lesson on filling in forms and their interpretation, words on forms that my lot may not understand and letter presentation. I also threw in a bit on how to speak to people. That jumped-up little prick annoyed me as soon as he entered my classroom.' Mick suppressed a smile, never having heard Mel speak like that. 'He had an air of arrogance.'

'Well, Mel, what did you say?'

'After he'd told me that what I was teaching wasn't relevant, I asked him if he'd taught in a dockland school for forty years and how would he prepare his pupils for life outside. I asked him how his skills and qualifications would benefit my pupils. I also told him what I told you many years ago, that our success is measured in different ways, just look out of the window to see that.'

'Did you know that girl Susan Watson was passing your class and overheard all that?'

'No,' Mel answered.

'She told him to leave and told him that you were the best teacher in the world. Come on Mel, I'll take you home.' Mel got in the car with flowers, wine, cards, books and memories. 'We'll see you tomorrow night, Mel.'

Tomorrow night became tonight. Mel arrived at the school hall. The place was transformed. Mel wasn't keen on fuss but was happy with a small group of staff in familiar surroundings. Everything went to plan. Mel was comfortable with the atmosphere and enjoyed the whole evening. There were short speeches, a presentation, and Mel thanked everyone for helping her through a happy career. She was dropped off at home with yet more cards and gifts.

Mel fleetingly thought about her own family who had virtually ignored her over the years. She hadn't turned out to be the 'posh daughter'. There was very little contact now, and even that was not always pleasant.

Within days of retiring, Mel was in the Lake District, walking, taking photos, painting. She loved her new life, freedom and flexibility. She very soon got out of the way of working. She learnt new skills, and in many ways she felt like she'd been born again. She did things she'd never done before. She visited the Scottish Islands, went on wildlife tours and painting holidays.

Mel also enjoyed being at home. She had a new kitchen fitted. She loved her work in the community with the homeless and Narcotics Anonymous.

Summer turned into winter. Mel loved the social scene of concerts, bands, and films. She felt young again in retirement. She was in regular contact with her work colleagues. Life was just so fulfilling and happy.

*

Mel's mate dropped her off in the ward at the local hospital. It was a day unit. It was a daft thing to do to get that glass stuck in her hand. The sister had a calm, kind air of efficiency. 'Mel, isn't it? I think someone here would like to admit you and if it's alright with you she'd like to use you as a module for day care.'

'Jenny,' Mel whispered. The student nurse hugged Mel.

'I'll leave you two,' the sister smiled.

'Jenny, I couldn't have wished for anyone nicer.'

'Don't be all day,' Sister shouted across. 'I know you two have plenty to talk about.'

'Jenny, update me. It's me that gets into trouble now, not you,' Mel smiled.

'Can I call you Mel now Miss?'

'Yes, yes,' Mel replied.

'Mel, do you remember I told you me mam had me when she was fifteen and she kicked me dad out and told me to get a better life than her. Well, me mam died three months ago. She cried when she saw me in my uniform. They say hard work doesn't kill anyone but it killed her.'

'I'm so sorry to hear that.' Mel was silent for a moment, saddened by this news. 'Jenny, your mam died knowing that your life will be better than hers.'

'Get on with that admission, Jenny.'

'Sorry, Sister.'

'Jenny, you're the teacher now. What happens next?'

'Oh, Mel, I'm coming to theatre to stay with you. The X-rays show the glass is near to your median nerve so they have to use ultrasound control. It's all done under local anaesthetic.'

'You've done your homework, Jenny,' said Mel, impressed.

Jenny disappeared.

'Sister, I taught Jenny.'

'She's one of the best students I've ever had,' stated the Sister.

Everything went to plan and Mel was ready for home.

'Jenny, would you like to come with me to Narcotics Anonymous. It might help you in your carreer.'

'Oh, Mel, I'd love to.'

'Good. I will ask Sister and you can let me know the outcome.'

A few days later Mel's phone rang. It was Jenny. 'Mel, the School of Nursing said if I keep a record of my hours with you I can put it towards my placement!' Mel couldn't help smiling to herself. She remembered when she had been at Jenny's stage of life, choosing her career, looking for something that would fulfil and excite her. She'd chosen teaching, and had devoted her life to it. Here was Jenny, about to embark on the same adventure, and Mel had no doubt that Jenny would go on to save many lives. Perhaps one day in the distant future, at the end of Jenny's career, she'd meet a young person she'd once helped, and the cycle would start over again.

Illusions

Ray Stewart

It started with an argument. I can't remember what it was about, but it was probably trivial.

As a result I went to the school PTA meeting on my own. This was unusual as we both, as a rule, attended the functions at our respective schools. It was an entertaining evening where supposed barriers between teachers and parents were not apparent, ending with some game which involved racing around the hall and being eliminated.

I drove home with the thoughts of the forthcoming six weeks holiday. We were going to a cottage on the Llewyn Peninsula, within striking distance of most of the narrow gauge railways in North Wales.

I parked the car and walked up the path to the back door. Tec sensed me coming and barked to greet me. He would be wanting his late night walk before long. Linda was sat where I had left her, her face drawn and non-committal. 'Argument to continue,' I thought, and sat in the chair by the window. She suddenly erupted into tears, running across the room to hug me.

'Don't worry,' I said. 'It was only a daft argument.'

She looked up into my eyes. 'No,' she said. 'Your Dad's been on the phone. Your Mam's got cancer. At best, she's got twelve months to live.'

I sat down numb, but with my brain whirring.

'Perhaps they're wrong,' I said, perhaps to comfort myself as much as her. 'Doctors are only human and can make mistakes. Perhaps they've got this one wrong.'

The rest of that evening was a blur of emotions, as were the remaining days of that summer term.

I spoke to Dad the following day and he told me that he wanted my mother to enjoy her remaining months as much as possible and so he did not want her to be aware of the seriousness of her condition.

We were off to Wales a day or two later, so we popped into Mam's pub, The Cliff, to see Mam and Dad. It was unreal. She seemed to be as she always had been, strong, vital and bloody-minded. It only helped to reinforce the illusion that the doctors had got it wrong. That Friday was my last day at John Bosco's and after the presentation, a tracksuit embroidered with the school name, I drove down to Linda's school to pick her up. She was busy somewhere so I waited in the staffroom. When she entered I burst into tears, I think because I was leaving somewhere where I had been very happy, but ... a third promotion in four years was not to be sniffed at. That Friday night we raided Makro for holiday essentials, notably, bottles of Villa Sarsaparilla, tins of dog food for Tec and the Tommy LP by The Who. Linda tried on a brown maxi-coat and fell in love with it. It was eighty pounds and while she was looking at the records I popped it into the trolley. Well ... We were on reasonably good money with the pair of us teaching.

Returning home we packed the bags whilst copying the 'Tommy' LP onto tape so that we could enjoy it in the car when travelling.

The holiday was pleasant. Tec loved the large garden behind the cottage whereas we tended to avoid it as it seemed to be impossible to walk across it without hearing the crunching of snails beneath our feet.

When walking into Rhiw, the nearest village, it was a little disconcerting to hear the locals, who were quite happily chatting away in English, suddenly continue the conversation in Welsh. I wondered what they were saying about us.

We'd had a job finding the village in the first place pre sat-nav, stopping to ask an old man at the side of the road, who helped us in a lilting Welsh voice, 'Why I know no place better. It was where I spent my childhood,' before directing us down an overgrown lane.

When we returned we brought Mam a stainless steel engraving of 'Mountaineer', one of the

Ffestiniog locomotives. She seemed to be her usual self, despite going for treatment that knocked her sideways. The illusion persisted that all would be well.

The next few weeks of the school holiday were rather hectic. It was the 150th anniversary of the Stockton and Darlington Railway and engines from all parts of the country were arriving in the north east for the celebration cavalcade. We had a friend, Norman, who was a signalman at Darlington North Box, and he had access to all of the loco movements. It became a common event for the phone to ring, and we'd be sent off to some location identified by Norman, with cine camera and tape recorder to hand. One memorable occasion occurred about midnight, when he rang to tell us that 'Morayshire' and the 'Caly' tank were due through Durham within half an hour. We hurried there just in time to watch it cross Durham viaduct with the whistles of both engines wide open. The hairs stood up on the back of my neck as I listened to that sound which was preserved on the tape recorder.

The cavalcade itself was an anti-climax. We camped beside the line at Heighington and recorded the occasion on cine film. The noble locomotives reminded me of wild circus animals trained to perform for an audience.

It was soon time to return to school and the normal term time routine began again, only this term there seemed to be more visits to Roker to see Mam and Dad. They had left The Cliff and moved to Melrose Gardens, a couple of streets away from the pub. Dad had become angry one day when he found Mam in bed 'doing the books' because the relief manager was incapable of doing them. The result was that in what seemed to be an inordinately short time, he had bought the bungalow and moved Mam into it, away from her last pub. Her condition was visibly deteriorating although it did not appear to be happening too rapidly. She was now commuting between hospital and home and she no sooner arrived at one of these destinations that she decided that she wanted to be at the other. Her most effective pain relief could only be administered at the hospital; the pain relief for use at home appeared to be largely ineffective. I remember her getting silently angry at Dad one day, after he had brought her a game with a popomatic dice to pass the increasing amount of time that she was spending in bed.

'Look what the silly bugger's bought me.'

She never told him though.

We hardly seemed to go home. The routine was work, Melrose Gardens, home late at night, and work again. One Sunday one of my mates from the Gresley support team arrived at my mother's and told me that the 'Scotsman' and 'Mayflower' were double-heading[1] through Durham later that

---

[1] railway term meaning two locomotives coupled together for the purpose of providing additional traction to haul a train

afternoon. I was torn. I felt guilty about even wanting to go but Linda smiled at me and told me to go, promising that she would stay with Mam until I returned.

And so I stood on Newton Hall Bank and filmed the splendid sight, so common in my childhood ... only this time no hairs stood up on the back of my neck. Only tears ran silently down my face.

Christmas was surreal. My mother was the youngest of nine children and the surviving members all turned up on Christmas day. I suppose they wanted to say 'Goodbye'.

The early months of the new year saw an increasingly rapid deterioration. We spent more and more time at Roker or the hospital until the final day.

It was a grey Sunday in March. We were getting ready for the daily hospital routine again. Linda looked drained so I suggested that I would drop her off beside the river, where she could spend a few hours with her colleagues from the sub-aqua club. She could come with me on my evening visit. Accordingly, I dropped her off on the way to the General. On arrival I found Dad sitting at Mam's bedside holding her hand. She was breathing irregularly. I think about two or three large laboured breaths per minute. I was later told by an uncle that at lunchtime she had been screaming with the pain, and that they had pumped her full of drugs to give her some comfort. On reflection I believe that Mam had been given a deliberate overdose. She had been given enough drugs to kill the pain ... but also enough to kill the patient. I am grateful to the person responsible. I looked at Dad and said, 'I'll be back.'

I drove down quickly to Roker beach and, seeing the sub-aqua club boat between the piers, flashed the car lights to attract their attention. Eventually someone rowed Linda ashore and as she lifted her worried face towards mine I said quietly, 'It's time.' We drove back and sat at Mam's bedside in silence watching the slow labouring breaths which became less frequent.

I left briefly to go to the toilet and the thought crossed my mind that I should tell Linda's parents, Ronnie and Renee, who lived only a few hundred yards away. I reached the corner of Kayll Road and Chester Road, less than a hundred yards away from my destination, but then something made me turn back. I was in time to see one or two more laboured breaths and then they stopped. 'She's gone,' I said, and went to fetch the nurse. It was twenty minutes past seven. Hospital routine took over. We were ushered into a side room and screens were placed around the bed. Her belongings were gathered up in a clear plastic bag and given to me. I looked at the sad little items. A lifetime summed up in a plastic bag.

We returned to Melrose Gardens in silence and on entering the house I bent down to light the gas fire. I turned to face Dad and Linda, to see Linda pointing frantically at the fireplace. I glanced behind and then stepped in front of the clock. The clock ... That hideous clock flanked by two leprechauns had been brought back from Ireland some years previously, and had stopped at twenty past seven.

'I suppose we'd better have a cup of tea,' I said and Linda led Dad into the kitchen. I turned, winding the clock up and on.

I never shed a tear. To be honest it was a relief that she had died. At least her suffering had come to an end. We both took time off work to look after Dad and make arrangements. To those who knew us, I was the one who was cool and in control. Work told me to take as long as I needed. Linda was docked three days pay. Fuck the caring catholic education system.

I registered the death and made the arrangements for the funeral and I seemed to be the only one unaffected. Before the funeral I went into the bedroom where she was lying in an open coffin. I sat next to it and said something long lost to memory. We had been very similar in character, bloody-minded and stubborn, and it must have been the first time I got the last word in. I kissed her forehead. It felt like cold porcelain, and taking one last look, left the room.

The funeral was a long drawn-out Requiem Mass filled with words of discomfort, followed by interment at Mere Knolls Cemetery. Later in the afternoon I left the 'celebrations' to referee a schools football semi-final. I had been asked to do this some weeks previously and although I had been contacted to see if I wished to withdraw because of the circumstances, I had said that I would still referee the game. It was a return to some sort of normality.

I showed no emotion during my mother's illness or at her death. It was not until some five or six weeks after the funeral when I took Tec out for his long walk. I must have been longer than usual for Linda came out in the car looking for me. As she pulled up alongside me, Tec was trotting at my heels, and my face was full of tears. The last illusion was broken.

Mouldywarp

Tamsyn Naylor

The earth was warm, the early morning sun had taken the dew off and steam rose up around the fern fronds. The ground was soft and crumbly as it started to heave; like an egg frying in a pan, it lifted and sunk and lifted again. The crumbs of soil started to roll down the hummock as a sharp claw surfaced, followed by a soft velvety body. It paused for a moment and then dived back into its burrow, continuing to scrabble into the new ground. As he advanced, loam scouring past his shoulder towards the now obscured light, sinuous, fibrous strands fell out of the loose material. Thinking it was his prize, a juicy earthworm, he bit into it expecting to taste the meaty goodness of his favourite morsel. Instead he got a slightly bitter taste. Carrying on digging, he started to feel slightly strange, light headed and relaxed. Stopping his endeavours he panted, thinking tiredness was taking over, but it was light, a brightness opening up in his head. The tunnel started to illuminate; colours appeared in the gloom, the sides of the tunnel felt wavy as he leaned against them to steady himself.

He had struck gold. The fine strands were fibres formed by fungal growth, rich in energy, and hallucinogenic.

As he relaxed against the passageway, the space seemed to open up and the ceiling fall away, coloured light came flooding in. Invigorated with energy and eager to find more fibres, he scrabbled further into the soil, feverishly opening out more tunnels and back-digging the soil onto the surface. All morning the ground heaved with his efforts, until the surface of the grass resembled goose bumps on cold winter skin.

He had made a cavern, but found no more fibres; his buzz was only for the short term today.

Having returned to his sleeping quarters for a well-earned rest, the mole slept soundly. The walls of the chamber had old coins set into them, some with the king or queen's head smiling down. The floor was studded with broken pieces of blue and white patterned pottery.

That evening he returned to the new cavern. On surfacing, the moonlight was shining down over the disturbed field. A badger passing by snuffled into the clearing. He cast a disapproving glance to the mole, remembering the damage that had been done to the east part of his sett some winters ago, by the stupidity of the father of Mouldywarp, letting water from a nearby stream flood several passageways of his sett and undoing months of toil in his expansion scheme.

Innocently, Mouldywarp told Brock of his discovery in the passageway.

'Yes, boy, there are a few strands to be found if you are lucky.'

'Do you know where there is more?' he politely asked of the rugged grey, wise, whiskery face.

'Not near my place,' he gruffly barked, making a sniffing gesture as he continued on his trail.

The next evening the mole had surfaced and was grubbing on a few leatherjackets, when a strange dull thud disturbed the quiet of the woodland edge. He paused, hidden in the bramble cover, watching. Big Ones were moving around in front of two white light beams, talking in muffled tones, while they pulled out a bouncy snakelike coil. The mole was still, the men unaware they were being watched. The coil was rolled out and pulled across the ground but, in the startling beams of light, Mouldywarp could not see clearly what was happening, so wandered on. He continued to hear muffled conversation between the Big Ones for some time. The stillness of the setting was broken when an unnatural hum, turning into an enormous vibrating purr, bounced around the space, startling a blackbird up into the sky in frenzy.

There would be no chance of a good meal with the commotion so the mole scrabbled back towards one of his tunnel entrances. His whiskers twitched as he brushed past the vegetation, but... a sniff, another sniff, strange ... bitter ... powerful ... poison.

He became alert; his most powerful senses picked up the distinctive smell and he knew it would bring fear. It was the badger's sett the end of the coil ran into and the badger that would be in danger.

Mouldywarp scurried back to his tunnel and scrambled along the subterranean roads into the area he knew the badger sett abutted. He could sense, by the vibration of his activity, where the tunnel wall was thinnest and started to claw at the wall. He easily broke through, turning into the descending tunnel and darting further into the depths. A few seconds in and he could hear commotion, squeals and panic-stricken cries. The two cubs, still pink-skinned and innocent, did not know what to do. They just pinned themselves against the back wall of the chamber in fear. The fumes were well infused throughout the cavern so the mole pushed the youngsters back the way he had come. It took some effort to persuade them to come with him but they had not seen the sow for some minutes past. Regaining fresher passageways, the mole felt a massive thunder of sound, followed by a blow to his side as the huge mass of the panicky sow barged into him. She made a grab at the cubs, bustling them to her as she pushed her way further from the infected tunnels. On regaining the surface beneath a large arching beech tree, its base scratched with years of scrabbling, the sow turned and looked for the mole.

'I thought I had lost everything! What with Brock out hunting and the cobs all out of my sight. Thank you. I can't thank you enough,' she beamed, her eyes squinting in pride.

'It was nothing. Just felt something was wrong,' Mouldywarp replied.

'You have been so kind to us,' she said. 'How can I ever repay you?'

'I do not ask anything of you, after all we are good neighbours,' the mole said softly.

*

The next evening there was a soft rain falling in the clearing when the ground once again heaved and pulsated to the efforts of the excavator. As he surfaced, he was startled to find the badger waiting next to his tunnel.

'You know lad, you should not dig in this place, the ground is too stony. Try over there,' he said, indicating the woodland where the core of his sett lay.

A huge beam of satisfaction crept across Mouldywarp's face as he realised what this meant.

He returned to the cavern he had made and burrowed towards the wood. He had hardly advanced twenty body lengths when the familiar strands appeared in the roof. He opened out a comfortable space, big enough to turn around in before chewing into the moist strands. As the cavern lightened, the mole reclined and let the warmth of the rainbow take over his mind.

The Lemon Tree

Josephine Esterling

Five-year-old Jessica watched her grandmother put each lemon into its little net bag and hang it on the mug tree that she kept on the window sill. 'Gran, why do you hang the lemons on there?'

'Aha love, you're a bit young to understand, but the lemons are a bit like life: sour, but good with a bit of sugar and made into lemon meringue pie. Do you fancy helping me to make some?'

'Oo yes please, that's my favourite. Can I have some for my best friend Sarah?' Jessica asked.

'Of course you can. How is she? Have the spots gone yet?' the grandmother asked.

'Nearly, she's got a big scab on her nose and it makes her look funny,' Jessica laughed.

'You didn't look very nice when you had chicken spots either,' the grandmother chuckled. 'Lemon meringue pie will cheer Sarah up. You can take some over to her later.'

*

'What's up love?' the grandmother asked when

eight-year-old Jessica came into the kitchen and sat quietly at the table. The grandmother could see that her granddaughter had been crying.

'She had a bit of a falling out with Sarah at school today,' her daughter said, coming into the kitchen and switching on the kettle.

'Gran, she's friends with Emily now. She called me names and everything,' Jessica said angrily.

'They have been friends for such a long time. Mum, do you think we should have some lemons off the lemon tree?' the daughter said. The grandmother nodded. She got up from the table and took a lemon from the mug tree on the window sill. She sliced the end off and passed it to Jessica.

'Yuck!' Jessica said.

'Good and sour,' the grandmother laughed. 'Now, you suck on that for a bit and we will think of something to make with the lemons.' She winked at her daughter and cut another two slices. The two women sat back and sucked the juice from the fruit. 'It's so sour, Gran,' Jessica said, pulling a face.

'Just like you and your best friend, all gone sour. Now, how does lemon drizzle cake sound?' the grandmother said.

'Yes, but that's not going to fix things between me and Sarah,' Jessica said sadly, with tears in her eyes.

'Now then, don't you worry about her, I bet you make a new friend by the end of tomorrow or I'm not your gran.'

Jessica and her grandmother made lemon drizzle cake and Jessica took two pieces to school the next day.

Jessica sat eating her packed lunch with the other children. Just across the table a girl eyed the two slices of cake wistfully. Jessica smiled. She had not seen her before. 'Hi,' she said, 'would you like a cake?' The girl nodded. Jessica passed a piece over to her. 'My name's Jessica. What's yours?'

'Alice,' replied the girl. 'This cake is lovely.'

'My gran and I made it yesterday. The lemons came off the lemon tree,' Jessica said.

'Do you grow lemons?' Alice asked, her mouth full of cake.

'No, but my gran has a mug tree that she hangs lemons on. Would you like to play outside with me and I will tell you about it?' Jessica finished her piece of cake and got up. The two girls went out to the playground.

*

Jessica sobbed at the kitchen table. 'Oh Gran, how could he do that to me?' Her teenage heart felt as though it was breaking.

'Oh love, I know it hurts and it feels like the end of the world, but that's all part of growing up.' The grandmother put her arm around Jessica. 'Teenage boys fall in and out of love as fast as they change their socks. You are a lovely girl and I am sure a nice young man will come along one day when you are a bit older, and he will turn out to be the one that you marry. In the mean-time, the other boys will be the ones that you learn about life from. Now, you go and get a lemon off the lemon tree and cut a slice for your mum and I, and one for yourself and we will see what we can make with the lemons.' Jessica dried her eyes and did as her grandmother asked.

'Mum, where did you get the idea for the lemon tree from?' the daughter asked.

'Well, many years ago, when I was still quite young,' the grandmother looked at her daughter, 'and your mum was a toddler,' the grandmother smiled at Jessica, 'an old lady put three lemons in my hand. Your dad – your Grandpa – and I were going through a bad patch at the time. She said that everything would be alright if I grew a lemon tree and made something sweet with the lemons. After all, she told me, you can always make something sweet from something sour if you add a little sugar. And, she was right. I made lemon cheese cake, your Grandpa's favourite and he came right back and said he was sorry and, well,' she winked at Jessica, 'you can guess the rest. Anyway, I did try to grow a lemon tree but they kept dying. Until, one day I had an idea and the lemons have been hanging on the mug tree ever since and, when things are a bit sour, I make something sweet and everything seems to work itself out just right. Now, shall we make lemonade? It will be nice and refreshing; it's very warm today. We could take it out to the garden and see if my new neighbours are about. They have a very nice son about your age, Jessica.'

Among the Flotsam

Antony Wootten

The gentle waves hissed like elegant ball gowns on delicate ladies. It was early.

The tide retreated slowly, its work done, its deliveries made: driftwood from a pirate ship, green kelp freshly selected from Neptune's garden, and a mermaid's mirror. It left them in a neat line halfway up the beach, dividing wet sand from dry.

This part of the beach was deserted, as it always was so early in the morning. Even during the hottest days not many people bothered to venture down here; being away from the main attractions of the funfair and the town centre it was usually quiet and empty, save for the few visitors who craved isolation and peace. Here, the golden sands could remain untouched for days, like virgin snow, and the dust devils and white horses and laughing spirits of the wind could play and dance unnoticed. So it was unlikely that anyone would discover the thing which the sea had mislaid.

The head lay still, propped at a slight angle on

the sand as though it were deep in thought. From a distance it looked like a bundle of seaweed, or a discarded bag; no-one would assume it was a head. As the tide retreated, the town was just coming to life.

The funfair too began to live. Music and voices drifted down on the wind which distorted them and tangled them so that from this lonely place they were nothing but a gentle babble like a stream tumbling over rocks, and the waves of the sea competed to drown them out.

The head seemed content to just listen.

A crooked man, old as ghosts, walked his dog along the beach. He was always here early, perhaps to beat the hustle and bustle of the day. He walked among the spiky grass of the dunes; the sand was firmer there and easier on ancient legs. But the greying sheep dog, old as she was, trotted happily along the soft sand of the beach, leaving deep paw prints behind her. She would often stop and sniff at something she found, digging like a happy child. As she sniffed, her master would amble on ahead, alone with his memories. The dog would wander far, forgetting herself sometimes, off across the wet sand which the receding waves had revealed; occasionally she would glance up to check on her master for reassurance: the crooked figure atop the dunes, dark today against the deep blue sky. As for the master, he just walked among the spirits of his past; at times his eyes would sparkle suddenly and he would smile to himself, and at other times his eyes would darken and he would shed a silent tear.

Today, as the man reminisced, the dog investigated the beach, following her curiosity, and her curiosity led her to the head. She sniffed, cautiously backed away, stalked it, growled; she crouched, ears back, chest flat to the sand, her swinging tail holding her rump high. It was tricky fixing eye contact with someone whose head was at such an angle but she tried, perhaps thinking it would get up and play if she stared pleadingly for long enough. But no, the head's empty eyes just stared back.

After a minute of confused stalking, a shrill and distant whistle whipped through the air. Seeing that her master was almost out of sight, the dog ran off, disillusioned. As she leapt into a run she scattered dry sand in the head's hair, but it didn't seem to mind. And now it was alone again.

In the hazy distance the fair was becoming lively, music and voices swirled in the summer air and memories were made. People splashed in the sea and laughed - or screamed - together. A little later, as the sun rose high and the pale moon too inched its way into the bright sky, two young people, a man and a woman, walked away from the noise of the fair to find a more secluded spot. They dropped their towels on the dry sand up near the dunes and ran down to splash around in the waves. They swam and bathed; they rolled and clambered over one another and they battled with great swords of water which they carved up from the ocean with a sweep of the arm, and then they scurried back up the beach again, splashing across the dark, wet sand, leaping the ragged band of flotsam, then churning the dry sand with their wet feet. They fell onto their towels and laughed, and as they held each other the distant waves chattered and spied, slowly reclaiming the wet sand. The head just watched.

After a while, the couple bundled their towels together and strode of through the dunes, laughing still, battling as they went. She was on his back as they dipped behind the grassy crest of the dunes but their voices lingered upon the sand long after the couple were gone from view.

The sun was high now, and the waves were clawing their way back up the sand, swirling into the footprints left behind by the beach's guests. Slowly, haltingly, as the hot day drifted by, they crept towards the flotsam until the soft bubbles were licking around the head, caressing it, gently washing away the sand which the dog had kicked across its cheeks and forehead, removing a strand of weed which had been draped across its nose. And then, as the tide rose, it lifted the head, gently, as though careful not to break its reverie, and carried it back out to sea.

In the distance, the big wheel turned.

Cupboard Love

Delphine Gale

Matilda-Cressida Hartley-Robinson sat down heavily on the edge of her bed, the August sun's cheerful rays quickly landing on her face and in no time at all making her hot and even more cross than ever. She was awaiting the arrival of her Aunt Jane and Uncle Rob, and their ever-expanding family. They had booked a holiday cottage in the country and were coming to take her away with them. Matilda was dreading it. She had been going on summer holidays with them for as long as she could remember, and was sure she used to like it, but now could hardly face the thought of two (please, not three) whole weeks of unmitigated cheerfulness and disorganisation, and the endless games she would have to play with the others. She heard a car pull up on the gravel drive and wearily dragged herself to her feet, pulled her bag towards her and with a last look at her bedroom, closed the door behind her and set off down the stairs to begin her ordeal.

The only child of an eminent scientist and a Government minister, Matilda had been unplanned, 'A contraception malfunction in a rare moment of passion between Edward and I, a mishap,' she had once overheard her mother telling someone. A rather inconvenient mishap, if truth were told, her father unable (or unwilling, Matilda could never be sure) to interrupt his research and his endless, endless papers published in all the important universities around the world. Streams of important people came to the house to see him. They were always ushered into his study and were often there for hours on end. Matilda did not always see them leave, and imagined that one day she would find the door unlocked and peep in there to see the place full of other scientists and doctors, all crammed in, sitting on each other's knees, hanging from every available space, waiting to speak to The Great Man.

Her mother, on the other hand, was marginally more accessible, when she wasn't in London ('Parliament is sitting darling, don't be tiresome, I can't possibly come back now. Ask Consuela to give you a cuddle'). Sometimes, when she was at home for constituency work, she would read Matilda a story. Only ever short ones, they always had to be short. At least there was a good chance of finishing these stories, without them being interrupted by a telephone call, Matilda had come to realise. Matlida longed for a brother or sister; all her friends seemed to have them, and when she had suggested it to her mother, her mother had looked horrified and said, 'Oh Matilda-Cressida, perhaps one day.' But one day never came and Matilda never forgot the look of horror on her mother's face. She overheard her mother relating the whole thing to someone on the telephone (Matilda's mother appeared to assume that all children under the age of about ten were stone deaf) saying, 'Career suicide, darling, out of the question. Did the White Paper go through?' And the matter was never again mentioned by either mother or daughter. It's just how things were.

One might have imagined, therefore, that Matilda-Cressida Hartley-Robinson would look forward to the company of her cousins during her summer break from boarding school, but Matilda found it more and more difficult, as the years advanced, to enjoy their company and join in their games. It was better than rattling around at home though, trying to amuse oneself while the Consuela hurried through her chores, muttering away in the thick Columbian accent to anyone who would listen. Which was usually just Matilda and it was not always what Matilda wanted to hear. 'Why do I have to look after you, Mateelda-Creseeda? You are a beeg girl now; you are ten years oold. Go and do the beeg girl theengs. I am not a nannee, I am the Housekeeper of thees place,' and so it went on. Matilda would sometimes just follow Consuela around until Consuela would say, exasperated by trying to answer the child's questions in her limited English, 'Caramba,' throwing her hands in the air, 'where are your friends?' Unable to get Consuela to teach her Columbian swear words to use at school, Matilda would give up and wander off.

Holidays with her cousins were also preferable to being at school, of that there was no question. She had been packed off to boarding school as soon as possible, aged seven, after numerous nannies, but the holidays were often a problem. Sometimes, she could stay at school, when they had exeats and such like, but for the long holidays she was shipped off back to her parents.

To their credit, these days Theresa and Edward Hartley-Robinson almost always tried to palm her off onto others of their friends with children of a broadly similar age for the duration. Matilda shuddered at the memory of the holiday at an exclusive resort in Crete when she was six, and all the other children were teenagers and treated her appallingly. She ended up with sunburn so bad her shoulders blistered which thankfully confined her to bed for the rest of the holiday thus getting her away from the teenagers who teased her mercilessly about everything from her name to the socks she wore. Not that she hadn't heard it all before, teasing her about her name in particular, but she didn't really need it on her holidays.

A new group of American girls had joined her school, whose rock star and celebrity parents no doubt had as little time for their offspring as

Matilda's had for her. This, in Matilda's eyes, gave them common ground in which to sow the seeds of friendship, but the girls were having none of it, considering themselves worthy of hobnobbing only with (minor foreign) royalty and not the highly intelligent daughter of someone they most likely would never, ever, hear of in the bubbles which they seemed to inhabit. They all had names like Strawberry-Sky and Heavenly-Harley, but no-one teased them.

'Oh well,' thought Matilda, as she clattered her bag down the stairs, 'here we go.' As she reached the bottom of the stairs, the chaos she had heard from the far-reaches of her bedroom enveloped her. Aunt Jane almost screamed, 'Tilly!' at the top of her voice and pushed through the throng of children to give her niece a hug and a kiss on the cheek. Aunt Jane's familiar perfume lingered with Matilda, and gave her a peculiar feeling she couldn't quite place. Tom, Matilda's eldest cousin, nodded at her across her hallway. He was 12, almost too cool for school and definitely too buzzing for cousins; he remained a little aloof and just perceptibly irritated by the melee. Alice and Poppy, at eight and nine and closest in age to Matilda, were having an argument about whose turn it was to play on the iPad when they got back in the car; and Lizzy, at three years old, was next to hug Matilda, albeit at knee height and nearly toppling the poor girl. Uncle Rob was refereeing the iPad argument without much success and it was threatening to escalate into all-out warfare. Uncle Rob abandoned his lost cause and came over to Matilda to take her bag.

'Tilly!' he said affectionately, 'what on earth have you got in here? Not test tubes, I hope,' he said with a conspiratorial wink and a wide, friendly grin. He then looked around furtively and said in a low voice, 'I say Tills, your mum's not about is she?' Matilda smiled back at Uncle Rob and shook her head, knowing that to shorten her name to Tilly was Luciferous in her mother's eyes, and Uncle Rob would have earned a stern rebuke. Consuela came to the door to say goodbye to Matilda and after much theatrical eye-dabbing and a brief rib-crushing hug, disappeared back inside the house. They all piled into the car and set off.

*

Matilda settled herself into her seat in the car and leaned against the window. The gravel drive and vaguely straggly garden passed her and she felt a slight pang of longing just to stay at home. With a sigh she pulled out her book and laid it on her lap, ready for later. Tom was playing on his newly-acquired phone; Alice had been ultimately victorious and was playing on the iPad and Poppy was talking to no-one, having taken defeat very badly indeed. Lizzy was talking to a weird, blue-coloured toy which Matilda thought was probably supposed to look like a person, though goodness knows who, and Lizzy explained who the character was. Lizzy, her golden curls and little dimples in her always-smiling face, chatted to Matilda until she became drowsy with the journey and dozed off. Eventually, and with some relief, Matilda sought refuge in her book. Order had been restored.

*

After what seemed like an eternity, the excitement level in the car increased as Aunt Jane announced, 'Nearly there, Troops!' It had taken a little longer than anticipated because Aunt Jane's map-reading skills left little to be desired, and there was almost a diplomatic incident when Uncle Rob finally lost his patience and, snatching the map, turned it round ('This way, Jane, we're travelling in this direction,') and finally rescued them from the winding country lanes ('It's a scenic route, Rob,' through gritted teeth). There followed a flurry of activity between Uncle Rob and Aunt Jane as they deciphered the holiday company's directions (very straightforward, as it turned out) and they pulled into the courtyard of the cottage. The car engine switched off, they all looked at the cottage for a moment or two, taking in what would, by the end of their holiday, be achingly familiar. Aunt Jane broke the silence.

'Well,' she said a little breathlessly, 'I was expecting a little cottage. This place is enormous!' Everyone climbed out of the car and gazed at the building. It had, at some time, been a barn, and all on one level. Then someone had come along and, if the windows in the roof were anything to go by, made it into a two storey cottage. Lizzy, sleepily balanced in Uncle Rob's arms, rubbed her eyes and said, 'I'll get lost in there!' The spell broken, everyone laughed and, retrieving the key from underneath the milk can by the back door, they all piled into the porch and on into the house.

*

Up to this point Matilda had felt somewhat indifferent to the whole affair. She didn't want to stay at home on her own for the summer, but equally she didn't want to be part of the whole 'family holiday' either. She didn't want to be lonely and miserable, but she didn't want company and happiness and games and fun. So what did she want? As they entered the house Matilda was taken by surprise at the cosy and welcoming feel of the place. From the porch, they entered the kitchen in which were all the essentials in for the grown-ups, and a fridge for Tom to raid and moan about when he'd emptied it. At the end of the long narrow kitchen were two doors, one straight ahead leading into a smaller room with a PlayStation in it, and the other on the left led into the dining room. The dining room had a big galleried staircase in it and took the whole family's collective breath away when they saw it. The walls were covered in heavy, floral wallpaper, but far from overpowering the space, made the whole place feel cosy and friendly. Matilda had the sensation that this cottage was greeting her with open arms. She had never felt anything like it.

Even Alice and Poppy had stopped their endless bickering to marvel at their new home for the next couple of weeks.

*

When all the bags had been unloaded, when the bedrooms had been chosen and settled into and when the grown-ups had drifted out onto the patio with a glass of wine in the early evening sunshine, the children wandered out into the huge garden to explore. Lizzy slipped her chubby little hand into Matilda's and said quietly, 'Please, Tilly, can I explore with you?' Matilda looked down at her cousin, her face now a little grubby and her eyes just showing signs of tiredness. 'Not really,' Matilda replied, a little unkindly. 'I'm off upstairs to read my book.'

'Oh,' replied Lizzy in a small voice, 'I wanted to explore with you more than anyone,' and she looked down at her new holiday sandals.

'Maybe tomorrow,' said Matilda, extricating her hand from the three-year-old's grip. 'Go and ask one of the others. They're all out here'

'No, it doesn't matter. Tom says I'm too little and a nuisance, and Poppy and Alice are putting up the tent and won't let me help.' She pushed her thumb into her mouth and sat down on the grass. 'Please, Tilly, I love you best.'

'Tomorrow,' Matilda called over her shoulder as she walked off to the house and upstairs to the bedroom chosen for her by the fact it was the only one left. She climbed the stairs, turned left through the little arch, up a few more stairs and, once through the upstairs sitting room, arrived at the bedroom door. She went in and closed it behind her. Matilda picked up the book she had been reading in the car and fell onto the double bed. She opened the book and started to read. The words remained stubbornly on the page. Hard as she tried, she could not make them fly into her head. She started the page again but with no success. She tried yet again but the words would not fly. Irritated, she slammed down the book and sighed. She looked around the sunny room. Might as well go and explore with Lizzy then, she thought crossly. She went back down stairs to find Aunt Jane with a tearful Lizzy in her arms, on their way to the waiting bath and then bed. Matilda felt dreadful; Lizzy was only a baby after all.

'I'm sorry, Aunt Jane, I was just coming ...' Matilda began but Aunt Jane just shook her head.

'Don't worry, Tilly, she's had a long day. I'm sure you can do something with her tomorrow.' Matilda was grateful and a little surprised at her Aunt's reaction. Matilda's behaviour was always being rectified or modified one way or another by her mother, teachers or Consuela, and she had really expected a sound telling-off for being so mean.

*

By the end of the first week the sun shone relentlessly and the family had been here, there and everywhere. The beach had been the favourite:

miles and miles of beautiful golden sand, decorated by a sapphire sea on one side, and jewel-bright beach chalets on the other. The sand, illuminated by the warm embrace of the summer sun, seemed to smile contentedly up at the indulgent azure sky. Cheery, busy little gossamer clouds popped by before hurriedly disappearing on more urgent business. Matilda looked at the scene and had never seen anything so beautiful, 'Like a horizontal funny kind of Christmas tree in summer,' she wrote in her diary. They had been to the seaside before, Crete even, but nothing compared to this. The gulls wheeling, screeching and calling, children screaming and laughing, the waves lapping lazily along the shore, daring and enticing you to partake of their pleasures. All of this wove itself into Matilda's mind, like a rich aural tapestry perfectly complimenting the colourful panorama. Sights and sounds, she thought, as the sand glittered through her fingers onto the smooth shells below. She wriggled her toes in the bath-warm water of the rock pool and felt the slime of the seaweed on the rocks. She breathed in the salty, fresh sea air, peppered occasionally by the smell of something cooking from the beach-side cafe. But still something nagged away at Matilda. Something missing, something, something.

'Tills!' she heard Uncle Rob say loudly. 'Tills! You're miles away, you goose. Take this ice-cream before it melts!' He laughed. Matilda ate her ice-cream and wondered what Uncle Rob would be like if he was really cross. She turned to see what Alice and Poppy could possibly be arguing about now.

'Malice and Poopy,' Uncle Rob called, 'ice-creams,' and the two girls forgot entirely their disagreement and turned their attentions to their father. Taking their ice-creams and using their free hands, the girls pummelled Uncle Rob until he fell to the sand in mock pain and begged them to stop. Aunt Jane made friends with some people close by and Lizzy played contentedly with two tiny dolls in a sandcastle made for her by Tom. 'These are my Princesses,' she said to Matilda, her little voice filled with awe and wonder. Rob sat down next to Jane and gave her a kiss on the cheek.

'Is it me, or is this just about as close as you can get to paradise?' he asked his wife, stroking her arm. 'Gem of a place, this, Jane. We'll have to come here again.'

'Hmmm,' answered Jane, a little distractedly, 'maybe organise a beach chalet next time. Rob, have you noticed how quiet Tilly is? Do you think she's ok?' Jane dropped her voice and glanced across to where Matilda was engrossed in her book. Jane could not bear the thought of having to telephone Matilda's parents and tell them she was ill.

'Well, she's eating,' replied Rob, who used this particular yardstick to measure a number of things from the likelihood of chickenpox to homework not having been done. 'Are you worried?'

'Well, frankly, yes, she's not usually as quiet as this. I might try to have a word with her later, find out if everything's ok at home. You know,' and she cast a sideways look at her husband, 'with things not being terribly conventional.' Catching his skyward roll of the eyes she continued, 'Come on Rob, we both know what that brother of yours is like, and Lady Theresa is too busy planning her route into Number 10 to even remember she has a child. Unless, of course, it's election time.'

'Jane, you are deeply unattractive when cynical,' he twinkled back at her. 'But I take your point. Try to get her by herself later, see what she says. Can't bear to think of her being unhappy. And I can't bear to ring her parents either,' he added, with a grin.

'I think she's sad,' came Lizzy's small voice. They didn't even know she was listening.

*

By the end of the first week the weather had broken. 'Looks like indoor games then,' Matilda thought to herself as she closed her book, now nearly finished, and turned off her light. With a bit of luck the weather forecast would be wrong and they would be able to go out somewhere, so that Matilda could be almost invisible again.

At the end of the first day of rain and thunder, the indoor games were wearing a little thin. Even Uncle Rob was losing his smile, tired of refereeing and suggesting and mollifying. As the children grew older it was becoming harder to find games which they would all play, and Rob and Jane were determined that their children would use the technology available to them in the palms of their hands alongside as many traditional pursuits as possible, for as long as possible. Tomorrow would take some careful planning, of that there was no doubt. So, at breakfast the following day, with a fine and miserable drizzle thwarting any outside plans, Uncle Rob suggested a trip to the local museum. A collective groan went up around the table and with brilliant timing, Matilda came up with a suggestion of her own before an all-out uprising took hold.

'Why don't we play hide and seek?' she said, quietly. 'The sun will be out this afternoon, we can go out then.'

One by one the children agreed, and Aunt Jane said she would help Lizzie. Tom was warming to the idea, as he always thought his hiding places were the best. The breakfast things cleared, they started their game. The house had lots of little hidy-holes: long, long curtains; the eaves cupboards; deep window sills and window seats where, if you pulled the curtains across just enough, you would never be found. Tom was the best seeker of the lot and he knew it. So did everyone else and there was much hushed excitement as they all chose their hiding places carefully. Tom must have as hard a job as possible, of that there was no doubt. Matilda and Tom had played together from birth, Aunt Jane often having been asked to 'babysit' Matilda while her parents did more important things. There had always been a strong, friendly rivalry between the two of them, particularly in games such as this. When it was Tom's turn, Poppy hid in the tiny cupboard under the stairs. The door did not fasten, and it had all the owner's cleaning things in it, but she squeezed in and sat silently, hardly daring to breathe. Alice climbed onto the low, wide windowsill in the little room off the kitchen, and pulled the curtains carefully across her. Lizzy and Aunt Jane laid as flat as they could under the quilt on Aunt Jane and Uncle Rob's bed, Uncle Rob making it as messy as possible to hide the lumps and bumps.

Matilda could not decide where to hide. She had used the cupboards in her bedroom; Tom would look there first. As she walked up the corridor towards the bathroom, she despaired of finding anywhere suitable. Then she saw it. The cupboard door where the central heating boiler was housed was just ever-so slightly open. Could she fit in? She peeped inside. It would be tricky, but she could just about manage it. She could see the sun just beginning to peep through the clouds and knew she would have to get a move on. She slid inside, and with her fingers in the gap between the floor and the bottom of the door, pulled the door close to. She didn't want to click it closed; Tom had the hearing of a bat and she would be discovered. She sat silently, waiting.

'Coming, ready or not!' Tom shouted from his bedroom. Matilda could hear him running around the house, looking behind furniture, tripping up over Uncle Rob's legs in his desperation to be the quickest 'seeker'. Equally desperate to be the longest undiscovered 'hider', everyone stayed as silent as possible. Lizzy was the first to break cover, unable to contain her excitement at the game and the increasing lack of oxygen under the bedcovers; her squeal of delight when he ran past the bedroom gave them away. Tom continued his search, eliminating hiding places that had already been used and, being somewhat forensic in his approach, quickly located Alice.

'Well, you're short,' he said bluntly, 'and you don't like spiders, so it had to be somewhere you could climb up to. Anyway,' he continued, 'the curtains in here are never closed. That gave it away, you dolt.' Alice gave her brother a sharp and surprisingly powerful elbow to the ribs before making veiled gestures as to where she thought Poppy might be. She was wrong, but Tom found her anyway ('I could see your red shoe sticking out, duh,') but Poppy thought Alice had given the game away and all hell broke loose. At the end of his tether, Uncle Rob shouted, 'Sun's out,' which was the signal for everyone to dash around wildly collecting their things to get in the car. Tom flew up the corridor to get his precious phone, and in doing so slammed shut the boiler cupboard door, trapping Matilda inside. At first she was so shocked she just sat there for a second or two. Then she knocked on the door.

'Hello,' she called, 'let me out!' Then, 'Hey, let me out!' at the top of her voice. But she could not be heard over the general desperation to get outside. No-one heard. Tom, having retrieved his phone, thundered past on his way to the car, shouting, 'Hang on, wait, don't you dare sit in my seat you cretin,' and before Matilda knew anything, the house was silent and she heard the car leave the drive.

Matilda sat in the dark. The handle on the inside of the cupboard was missing, and only now did she recall Aunt Jane catching her sleeve on the metal bit which protruded, cursing and saying, 'Keep an eye on that, it could be dangerous. Don't leave the door open.' 'Too late,' thought Matilda ruefully, 'too late for that.' And she sat there in the dark and dusty cupboard, unable to stand up, but sure that someone would come to her rescue soon. They did not. Matilda tried to turn the metal rod to open the door, but it would not budge. She pushed hard against the door, as hard as she could, but it would not move an inch. She realised the panels were thinner, and might easily break, so she kicked hard. The door was very stout, however, and determined to keep her prisoner. Stupid game, Matilda thought to herself, stupid, stupid game. And Matilda-Cressida Hartley-Robinson started to cry.

Matilda could not remember the last time she had cried, about anything. The hot tears rolled down her face, oblivious to her efforts to keep them at bay. They fell off her chin and landed on her tee-shirt, by now grubby from the dusty cupboard. She smiled wanly to herself as Consuela's voice popped into her head, 'In my country it ees a sin, a sin to have a cupboard with thees dirt.' The tears continued, and then it came to her. She remembered the last time she had cried. It was the first night of boarding school, when she lay alone in the crowded dormitory, and longed for the safety of her mother's arms and the comfort of a story, however short. Matilda had had to grow up very quickly then, and had been growing up ever since. She realised that she was crying because she had not been missed. However annoying Poppy and Alice were, they were certainly a presence no-one would forget, even if they wanted to. Who could forget Lizzy, when everyone wanted to cuddle and hold her and get one of her little smiles? How she longed for Lizzy's little hand in hers. And what about Tom? He would never be forgotten, he would not allow that. What had he shouted, at the top of his voice? 'Wait for me,' that's what, and they had. But they didn't notice Matilda was missing. Matilda felt a massive hollow in her stomach.

*

Jane and Rob were relieved to get into the car and out into the emerging sunshine. They would go to the National Park centre, they decided: outdoor things to keep all ages amused, little trails of varying sorts, and a tearoom. It was almost a relief to get out; hot as it was, rain was an unwelcome visitor making prisoners of them back at the house. Suddenly, Tom shouted, 'Oh bloody hell,' from the back of the car and Rob braked sharply.

'Tom! Will you please mind your language?' Aunt Jane said sharply, 'I will not have it! What on earth is the matter?'

'My phone has died and I need my car charger,' he snapped back. Then, more politely: 'Please, Dad, can we nip back to the house?' Exasperated, Rob turned the car around and they headed back to the house. Tom ran to the back porch of Waverley Cottage where he let himself in. The house was eerily quiet with no-one in, he thought. Momentarily he considered going into Poppy and Alice's room and hiding some of their things, but the effort required meant the thought stayed right there in his head. As he walked up the corridor, he heard a faint sound. He stopped, and listened. He heard it again, a little louder. He crept a bit further up the corridor. Was it a giant rat in his bedroom, bold enough now the house was quiet? He would soon put an end to its activities. A big stick was called for. Just as Tom looked round for a weapon, he drew close to the boiler cupboard. The sound seemed to be coming from in there! Very carefully and quietly he turned the handle and peeped inside.

'Cress!' he shouted. At that moment, Matilda lifted her head from her arms which were folded across her knees. Too busy crying, she had not heard Tom come back into the house. She turned her tear-stained face upwards and let out a gasp. It was difficult to say who was the more alarmed.

'Cress!' said Tom, more quietly, 'what the hell are you doing in here?'

'Hiding from you,' said Matilda, with a tearful grin, 'looks like I won, Jam.'

'So why are you crying?' he looked into her face.

'Because you all forgot about me. You didn't even miss me,' she wailed. Tom knelt down on the floor beside her. He put his arm around her shoulders and she sobbed. She could hear her mother's voice saying, 'If Mrs Pity-Me knocks on your door, don't let her in,' and Matilda sobbed a bit more. 'Oh Cress, I can't believe it. You shut yourself in this cupboard; it's a wonder you weren't gassed to death. It's a gas boiler.'

'Well actually, you shut me in,' Matilda said through her tears. The flood gates really had been opened. 'And the gas boiler isn't being used at the moment,' she added, to which Tom replied, 'But there could have been a leak; then you'd be dead.'

'No, I wouldn't, because I would have to be in here for quite a while I think,' she began, then they looked at each other and laughed a little.

'I thought you didn't want to be with us,' Tom said, 'you've hardly said a word to anyone this holiday. That's not like you, Cress.' He had called her Cress, or sometimes Egg and Cress, since they were very little and she in turn had called him Jam because he shared her surname. She sometimes called him Jam Roly-Poly when she wanted to really annoy him.

'Well, I was dreading it. I don't seem to fit in anywhere any more. Mummy and Daddy are too busy, I have nothing in common with the girls at school and you all get on so well together. Why would you want to trail me with you again this year? This is your family, Tom, not mine. You are so lucky.' Matilda had stopped crying now. 'Even Consuela doesn't want me around. I sound as though I feel sorry for myself, don't I?' Tom laughed.

'What's that thing your mum says about the woman at the door?'

'If Mrs Pity-Me knocks at your door don't let her in,' Matilda said in her mother's clipped tones, and they both laughed.

'Cress, it's great having you on holiday with us. Not this year, obv, you misery, but at least I don't have to listen to those two arguing ninnies when you're around. You're so much more, well, sensible.' Alarmed now at just how much cat had been let out of the bag with regard to feelings, Tom stopped. 'Look, all I'm saying is you're family,' he continued, a little more gruffly, now, ' and I for one am glad about that.'

'Thank you, Tom. I love being part of you all, you're all so much fun and normal and safe and happy. Even the ninnies.' She and Tom laughed at this. 'You are all the family I have and I was afraid that even you lot wouldn't want me around.'

'Well, I have to have someone to beat at hide and seek,' Tom said with a grin which totally mirrored his father's.

*

As they waited to set off once more for their afternoon's delights sampling National Park treasures, Jane and Rob let out a collective sigh.

'I do hope he gets a move on,' said Rob, ever so slightly irritated now.

'What's that, Lizzy?' Jane turned round to speak to her daughter.

'I said, where's Tilly?'

Jane and Rob looked at each other in absolute horror. Where was Tilly? Alice and Poppy had now realised Matilda was missing and began to cry. They imagined her standing at the roadside and having been abducted by a stranger; they imagined her alone in the house and accidentally starting a fire and burning to death; they imagined her running after the car when it set off and getting run over. They were sure Matilda was no longer alive and Jane had to say to them, 'For goodness' sake pull yourselves together. What on earth have you been reading to put these ideas in your heads?'

'It's just what Tom tells us,' they wailed, and held hands to comfort each other over their tragic cousin's assured demise. Everyone piled out of the car and ran into the house, to be met by Tom on his way out.

'Mum,' he said, 'I think you need to speak to Cress.'

*

Matilda had one last look at herself in the mirror. Hew new school uniform looked very smart indeed (and no hat! Imagine that!) and she straightened her tartan skirt for the umpteenth time. She picked up her bag and, closing her bedroom door behind her, raced off downstairs to eagerly await the arrival of Uncle Rob, Tom and Poppy and Alice.

'Are they here yet?' she asked Consuela, and without waiting for an answer opened the big front door. No sign. She was a little early, she knew that. Half an hour, to be precise, but she really couldn't wait for them to arrive. She went into the lounge to watch for the car. Matilda couldn't believe this was happening. Uncle Rob and Aunt Jane had had a summit meeting with Matilda's parents, poor Uncle Rob looking like a nervous wreck when they turned up. They had all been closeted away in her father's study for almost a whole afternoon, the initial raised voices giving way eventually to hushed and earnest discussion ('Parliament is sitting, darling'). Uncle Rob and Aunt Jane had emerged flushed and victorious, and after some tough negotiating had managed to secure Matilda a coveted place at Tom's (very good) state school and had even managed to persuade Theresa that two hyphens in any child's name was not the advantage she might have imagined. She had therefore, very reluctantly, agreed that Matilda would go to her new school, now aged 11, known as Tilly Hartley-Robinson. Matilda wondered if there had had to be a White Paper on the subject, and whether her father had had to publish some kind of announcement in The Lancet. Theresa had even been persuaded of the advantages of Matilda spending weekends with her cousins, as well as holidays. Matilda had expected her mother to put up some token resistance but she had readily agreed, 'It would certainly make life a lot easier.' Matilda could guess for whom.

She saw the car pull into the drive and, her big blue eyes shining with excitement, yelled, 'See you later 'Suela,' grabbed her bag and slammed the big front door behind her.

About The Authors

Antony Wootten moved to North Yorkshire in 2008, from London where he had lived and taught for more than a decade. In 2011, his first book, A Tiger Too Many, was published, and it was quickly followed by two more. Antony started the Grosmont Writers' Group in 2012, which was a great success, leading to the publication of the book you are reading now! Find out more at **www.antonywootten.co.uk**.

Paul Wootten lives in Berkshire, and so is an honorary member of the Grosmont Writer's Group rather than a regular attendee. He has recently had two novels for children published, and has a great many more lined up for future publication. Find out more at **www.beaufordhouse.co.uk**.

Josephine Esterling has spent many years moving around Essex but feels that in Grosmont she has found her true home. She fills her time, outside of working on the NYMR,with gardening, crafting, playing the clarinet and writing. Joining the Grosmont Writers' Group has given her an outlet for her abundant creativity.

Delphine Gale moved to Grosmont in 2011, having lived in the area all her life. In between looking after her family and renovating her house with her husband, joining the writers' group has helped her rekindle her passion for writing.

Paula Harrison has lived and worked in Yorkshire all her life. She is now semi-retired, and enjoys walking, especially on the moors, horse riding, and embracing life to the full.

Tamsyn Naylor has lived in Grosmont for most of her life and considers it her home. She is passionate about local history and geology, and writes many factual articles on these subjects. The Grosmont Writers' Group has inspired her to move out of her comfort zone and try her hand at fiction.

Ray Stewart is a retired teacher who came to work as a volunteer on the NYMR as a nineteen-year-old student. He is a little older than that now, still working on the NYMR, and writing in what little free time he has.

Caroline Stewart hails from Durham and is fiercely proud of her coal mining roots. She is an engineer and is passionate about music and singing, but writing fiction is a new venture. She lives in the beautiful hamlet of Esk Valley near Grosmont, and enjoys being part of the local community.

Melanie Allanson lives in Whitby but is originally from Sussex. She enjoys the hospitality of the north and has finally settled there after spending time working as a children's nurse in London, Manchester and New Zealand. Writing is a hobby that she fits around her three children. She has recently become a member of the writing group and hopes, in the future, to write a novel and give up the day job.

*

The Grosmont Writers' Group would like to thank their staunch supporters, Louise Wootten and John Harrison, who, despite not being writers themselves, attend each week, never failing to provide wisdom, insight, enthusiasm and great humour.

Books by GWG members...

A Tiger Too Many by Antony Wootten

Jill is deeply fond of an elderly tiger in London Zoo. But when war breaks out, she makes a shocking discovery. For reasons she can barely begin to understand, the tiger, along with many other animals in the zoo, is about to be killed. She vows to prevent that from happening, but finds herself virtually powerless in an adults' world. That day, she begins a war of her own, a war to save a tiger.

Grown-ups Can't Be Friends With Dragons by Antony Wootten

Brian is always in trouble at school, and his home life is far from peaceful. So he often runs away to the cave by the sea where he has happy memories. But there is something else in the cave: a creature, lonely and confused. Together they visit another world where they find wonderful friends, but also deadly enemies. Brian's life is torn between the two worlds, and he begins to believe that, in his own world at least, grown-ups can't be friends with dragons.

There Was An Old Fellow From Skye by Antony Wootten

A collection of Antony's hilarious limericks for all the family to enjoy. Featuring everything from King Arthur and his knights to inter-stellar space-travel, There Was An Old Fellow From Skye is packed with tiny tales which will tickle the ribs of children and adults alike.

The Yendak by Paul Wootten

Christer has shared most of his young life with his cousin Sophie. But when Sophie becomes desperately ill, his aunt hopes that the sound of Christer's voice might help to bring her round. He visits, as promised, and embarks on a quest for the mind of his cousin, lost somewhere in another dimension. Following clues in her diary he plunges into a strange world of oppressed people, ruled by the Yendak, a cruel and violent race. If they find him, he will never get back home.

Whispers on the Wasteland by Paul Wootten

Tim has spent the last few years of his life travelling from place to place, following his father's job. He rarely stays long enough to make any friends, and now he's come to Wattleford where a patch of wasteland is marked for development. A natural playground for the children, it has, over the centuries, sheltered humans and wildlife among its trees and shrubs. Tim finds himself strangely in tune with the peoples of the past, but the town council has plans to develop the wasteland. Modern machines bring destruction and change, and Tim and his father are all that stand in their way.

You can find out more at
www.antonywootten.co.uk.